To my parents, Jean and Damian Nadarajah, and my second set of parents; my aunt and uncle, Eva and Anton Nadarajah. Thank you.

To my younger brothers and sister, Jonathan, Derrick, Ian and Tania Nadarajah. Love you guys.

To Rico and Tyler... couldn't leave them out!

To Django

I can't believe that you REALLY think I ate a whole pizza! I DIDN'T!

Enjoy + spread the word!!

Delia

3

Kaia & Miella

I

Wiping off the beads of sweat dripping from his forehead, Kaia looked towards the portside of the boat his father and uncle had hired. The intense heat was too much for him to bear; all he wanted to do was return to his nice air-conditioned hotel suite and play with the new toys his parents had bought him. The last thing he wanted to do was be on a boring cruise which he knew would only be fun for the adults.

Looking around to find ways of entertaining himself, he spotted his cousin Miella. Annoying her was always fun, but this time she was too close to the adults for him to do anything without getting into trouble.

A stray, scrawny, ginger cat drinking water from a puddle on the floor of the wooden pier caught his attention.

"Miella, look over here!"

Clearly hearing Kaia, Miella decided to ignore him. She was grateful the two week family holiday was drawing to an end as he was the only person around her age she had for company and he was really getting on her nerves.

"MIELLA LOOK!"

With curiosity getting the better of her, she turned around to see Kaia standing at the edge of the pier with the cat scooped up in his arms.

Unlike her, Kaia was definitely not an animal lover. She immediately knew he was up to no good.

"The poor little kitty seems to be thirsty, I think I should throw him into the sea, that way he can drink all the water he wants!"

"You wouldn't dare! Stop messing around and leave the cat alone!"

"Don't tell me what to do, I'll do whatever I want!"

"You two! Move away from the edge before one or both of you falls in!"

Startled by the unexpected voice, they both turned around sharply.

"Zophia, Kaia is threatening to throw the cat into the sea!"

"Grass!" Kaia mumbled under his breath as Zophia approached them. Miella smirked.

Zophia-Eliane was a great friend of their parents, possibly in her late fifties although she was always vague about her age and never informed anyone of her birthday.

"Is that the truth Kaia? Were you planning on doing such a thing?" Zophia calmly asked.

"Of course not, Miella's lying again! She's always trying to get me into trouble!" Kaia played innocent.

"I am not!" Miella responded abruptly.

"That's enough! I don't want the two of you to start fighting over this. Kaia, leave the cat alone and step away from the edge! If either of you fell in, then at the very worst you could drown, and at the very least you'll have swallowed so much salty sea water that you'll be too ill to sail and ruin the last day of this holiday for everyone else!"

Kaia hated being told what to do. It always made him want to do the opposite, but as it was the last day of the holiday and he would soon be back home, he decided it would be more to his benefit to do as Zophia asked. As soon as he had placed the cat down he heard his uncle, Miella's dad, call out for everyone to get on board the boat. Miella ran straight over and joined the rest of the family. Zophia and Kaia followed closely behind. When Kaia reached the bottom of the boardwalk, he stopped. He could still vividly remember the sickness he experienced the last time they all went sailing and did not want to get on board. He decided that if he had to, then he was going to make sure he got something out of it!

"Kaia, what's the matter this time? Come on board please," his mother asked.

"NO!" Kaia screamed back, "I don't want to and you can't make me!"

Both fathers simply looked at each other and carried on with the necessary preparations for sailing. Child management, they felt, was not their job. They were both very successful business men who worked very long hours to earn their money. They wanted to enjoy themselves and not have a great holiday ruined by sulky children. Their wives, fully understanding this and also wanting the same, often bribed their kids to do what they wanted for an easy life! As a result they had two extremely spoilt twelve-year-old children.

Kaia's mother walked over to him. "Honey, we are not going to be able to spend much time on the yacht today as it is getting late and a little windy."

"That, *mother*, is exactly why I don't want to go! *I don't like it!*"

"Kaia, we are going home tomorrow and this is our last chance to see some of the islands, please don't ruin it!" She placed his hands in hers, lent over and whispered in his ear, "If you come on board then I promise you that as soon as you get to the airport you can choose anything you want from the shops and I'll buy it for you... ok?"

Kaia thought about this for a couple of seconds before replying. He wondered whether he should try bargaining for more. He decided it best to accept her offer as it was getting late and the sooner they started, the sooner they would get back to dry land. Stepping onboard, he overheard Zophia telling his mother that she should be much stricter with him. Kaia made a promise to himself to somehow get her back for interfering.

It certainly wasn't the biggest or the most luxurious vessel the children had ever sailed on but that was because they often had a crew working on board. This time their fathers had decided that as it was just a short cruise they would put their sailing skills into action and captain the boat themselves. Just the thought of this made Kaia grateful for the life jacket his mother insisted he and Miella wear.

Miella stood next to her father and smiled. She enjoyed sailing, but the real reason she was smiling was because she knew Kaia hated it, and was trying to think up ways of adding to his misery.

Just before they set sail, her father decided he wanted a photo to mark the occasion. He pulled out his camera and asked one of the dockworkers to take the photo. It was, of course, one of the latest digital models with the added function of producing instant photographs.

"Let me see it daddy, give it to me, *purleaze*," Miella asked, as soon as it was taken.

He looked down at his 'little angel', "Ok, but just as long as you promise to keep it somewhere it won't get wet or lost... not everyone has had a chance to look at it!"

"Ok daddy, I'll put it in a plastic bag first and then straight into my bag. I promise to look after it until we get back home to London and then I might give it back to you."

Her father laughed. "Ok, Miella, you do that, I trust you."

Miella looked at the picture; everyone was smiling in it, including Kaia! Her mother and aunt looked as beautiful as always and her father and uncle relaxed and happy. Although she would never admit it to him, she even thought Kaia looked quite sweet.

People often commented on how similar they looked for cousins. Miella couldn't see it herself but put it down to the fact they both had their mothers' bright blue eyes combined with honey-brown complexions which came from their fathers' side as Kaia's dad was from Trinidad and hers from Sri Lanka.

Looking at the photo again, she noticed an odd expression on Zophia's face. Her eyes didn't seem quite right. It was as though they were hiding a secret. Despite Zophia's uneasy look, the photo would have been almost perfect if it wasn't for the fact that in the horizon the blue sky had some odd bits of grey in it. Miella looked up but could only see a clear bright blue sky with some snow white clouds dotted about. Putting the photo in her bag, she just put the grey down to a possible fault with the camera and made a mental note to show her dad later.

II

It was getting late but for some reason the sky was much darker than what would be normal for an early evening. Kaia had fallen asleep below deck, in the cabin. Miella remained with the rest of her family. Watching them, she couldn't help but giggle as her uncle deliberately steered the boat over some rough waves, causing her father to miss the glasses that he was trying to pour champagne into. Although she found it funny to watch, the motion was causing her to feel queasy. She had never experienced sea-sickness before, but for the first time understood why Kaia hated sailing.

She called out to her uncle to ask him to stop, but he and the rest of the adults were far too busy enjoying themselves to hear her. In an attempt to stop from actually throwing up, she went down into the cabin and lay down on the bed next to Kaia.

III

A sudden jerk of the boat awoke Kaia. Looking around he saw Miella stirring in her sleep and immediately knew something was not right as the boat was rocking around violently. Managing to muster up some courage, he climbed up onto the deck to see what was going on.

"MUM! DAD! I want to go back, I feel really sick!"

There was no reply.

"MUMMMMM! DAAAADD! I WANT TO GO HOME!"

Still no reply. Aware that the boat was leaning towards the right and the waves crashing forcefully, he ran back down into the cabin, "MIELLA... MIELLA WAKE UP!"

"Go away... I don't feel well!"

"WAKE UP! Something's wrong, I can't see anyone!"

Miella sat up and as soon as she did, she too noticed the boat's now even sharper tendency of leaning towards the right and knew straight away that this wasn't one of Kaia's pranks.

"Stay there, don't move!" She yelled, running up to see for herself. The waves continued crashing fiercely on deck and the heavy downpour of rain from the dark sky terrified her. She turned back to look at Kaia and noticed the water starting to fill up the cabin below.

"MUM, DAD... SOMEONE... HELP US!"

Realising she couldn't wait for an answer, she sprinted back down the stairs and into the cabin. Kaia looked terrified!

"Kaia, listen! I can't see anyone else. We have to get on the life raft. If the others are over board, we'll have a better chance of finding them."

Kaia didn't want to leave. He was too scared, but knew he had to do as Miella said.

They both clambered back on deck and found the plastic case containing the life raft. Kaia held the case steady. Miella tried with all her strength to pull it open to get the raft out. The rough conditions were doing their best to make this an almost impossible task. Eventually managing to get the raft out, she pulled the cord to inflate it but just as she did, a strong gust of wind blew it straight into the sea. Both she and Kaia instinctively jumped into the water after it. She was the first to grab hold of this cord, and to her relief, Kaia appeared beside her to help pull it closer.

They were finding it extremely difficult to keep hold and at the same time keep their heads above water as the constant rough and choppy waves were starting to tire them. Eventually the pair managed to get the raft close enough to try and climb on board. Reaching out first, Kaia grabbed hold of the side. Miella keeping hold of the cord in one hand, somehow succeeded in pushing Kaia up with the other. He crawled on board and with all the strength in his body pulled his cousin up. They both collapsed on the raft from exhaustion, coughing and spluttering because of all of the salty sea water they had swallowed. Kaia looked over at his cousin.

"We... can't... give... up," he muttered, whilst trying to gasp for air. "We have to... keep on looking... for everyone."

"You're right! Blow on the whistle," replied Miella.

They both reached for the whistles attached to their life-jackets and with all the strength in their bodies tried to blow on them. But as their bodies weakened, the whistling gradually became inaudible.

IV

The storm eventually passed leaving them soaking wet and drifting along. Miella reached out towards Kaia and placed her hand on his arm attempting to comfort him. She didn't have the strength to speak. She had no idea as to how long they had

11

been on the life raft for and despite feeling weak and nauseous, she was still intent on trying to find their parents.

Raising her head slowly, the upper half of her body automatically followed. She noticed Kaia's eyes observing her movements but his body remained motionless.

Spotting something in the distance, she tried to decipher whether it was land or just the sun playing tricks on her. The bright sunlight reminded her of the photo her father had taken with the grey in the background. She now deeply regretted not saying anything at the time.

Remarkably the bag containing the photo had remained around her neck. She hadn't bothered to take it off because she had never intended to fall into such a deep sleep. Remembering her promise to her father, she was now even more determined to return his photo to him.

"Kaia, look up, I think I can see land!"

Kaia attempted to do so, but was far too weak.

"Kaia, please try," begged Miella.

Stretching his hand out towards her, they somehow managed to hoist his body up for him to see over the side of the boat.

"Miella, you're right," he mumbled.

As the boat drifted closer to the shore they saw a fishing boat approach. Relieved from the knowledge that help was on the way, they both sunk back into the boat and succumbed to their fatigue.

... ...

Appie

I

For a brief moment whilst waking up, Miella thought she was at home, having dreamt one of the worst nightmares possible! However, the pain she felt throughout her body and the hard surface she was lying on made her realise otherwise. She had no idea where she was but she was grateful to no longer feel the rocking of the boat. Afraid to open her eyes and face reality, she unwillingly resigned herself to the fact that she had no other option but to do so.

Taking a deep breath in, she decided to open her eyes on the count of three, *one…two…three…*

As her eyes adjusted to the light she noticed the room she was in was quite bare. From the inside, she was reminded of the log cabins she had seen in the old cowboy films her dad loved watching so much.

Miella wanted to get up and check on Kaia but the pain she felt worsened with even the slightest bit of movement. From where she lay she could see him lying down, and although not awake, she could see his chest moving up and down. At the very least, Miella took some comfort from seeing him breathe.

BANG!

A door slammed shut, followed by a kind of shuffling noise heading towards her. Terrified, she clamped her eyes shut. The noise continued past her and towards Kaia. If someone was going to hurt him, she had to stop them.

She opened her eyes.

Bent over Kaia, holding what seemed to be a glowing object in one of his hands, was a frail old man. Helplessly, Miella watched as he placed his other hand on Kaia's forehead and started mumbling something. Miella tried to hear what he was saying but he was talking in a language couldn't understand.

Kaia's body jerked suddenly. The back of his head was facing her. She couldn't see what was happening. Unable to move, Miella tried to shout at the old man, to make him stop, but her throat was too dry and sore for any sound to come out.

The haggard and scruffy old man had a similar milk chocolate brown complexion as her dad but the similarity ended there. His skin was much more wrinkly, weathered and rough, and his hair and beard were white and matted. She knew her father even in his old age would never look such a mess. Miella found his appearance pitiful especially as he was bare-chested and wearing really old worn-out shorts.

With a big smile on his face, and using a knobbly bamboo cane as a walking stick to assist him, he shuffled over to Miella and started to say something. Miella tried to reply. She wanted to tell him she couldn't understand, but there was still no sound.

Placing his right index finger on her lips, to tell her not to talk, he gently touched her stomach and head. The two places where she could feel the most pain. He moved the palm of his left hand roughly two inches away from her body. She immediately started to feel a soothing heat coming from it. He then quickly touched her stomach, throat and head. The pain she felt had now suddenly disappeared.

Miella was unsure if she was seeing things or if it was the reflection of the sunlight coming in from the window, but the old man seemed to have a mysterious glow of light coming from an object in his right hand as he healed her.

II

Opening his eyes and looking around, Kaia saw his cousin seated at a shabby little wooden table with a glass of water in front of her.

"Miella," Kaia whispered.

She turned around.

"Kaia, are you ok?" He looked at her and nodded. "Where are mum and dad?"

Miella's eyes started to well up with tears, one rolled down her cheek, "I still don't know Kaia! I wish I did…"

Kaia also wanted to cry but held his tears back. He knew deep down when they were on the boat that something bad had happened. He felt he had to be strong for both their sakes.

15

"Mimi, where are we?" Mimi was his nickname for her.

"Don't know! This place belongs to an old man who I think found us and has been looking after us. Kaia, I know this sounds crazy but I think he has special powers. He knew exactly where I was hurting and healed me without any medicine. And I saw him do the same to you!"

Kaia wanted to believe her but what she was saying was crazy. Unsure of how to reply, he was just about to try, when the old man walked in.

Kaia didn't know what to make of the old man; he looked far too old and weak to be of any danger to one of them, let alone the both of them. Still, Kaia thought there was something very odd about him and it made him feel uneasy.

The old man walked over to the children and in a strong accent said "Name?"

Miella responded but Kaia remained silent.

Looking directly at Kaia he repeated the question.

"None of your business!" Kaia replied bluntly.

The old man's gaze remained fixed upon Kaia but said nothing in response.

Kaia took in a deep breath, "My name is Kaia. Miella is my cousin. If you do anything to hurt us you will be in big trouble because our parents are looking for us at this very minute!"

The old man looked puzzled.

Miella looked angry and embarrassed, "Kaia... stop! He's looking after us, surely you must realise he's our only chance of finding them. Don't do or say anything to make him angry!"

"Name?" The old man repeated looking at Kaia before Miella had the chance to apologise.

"Kaia," he replied hesitantly.

"Miella... Kaia... Miella...Kaia," he repeated over again, almost as if to ensure he did not forget their names. Tapping the palm of his hand against his chest, he said "Appie."

Appie walked over to the cooking area of the hut; a corner of the room with a plank of wood attached to the wall, a sink with one tap and a weird looking oven type object made out of clay inside which a fire burnt. A sheet of metal lay on top of it. And on this, sat a metal pot containing some kind of soup Appie had made. Picking up the pot he walked over to the table where the children were seated and poured the soup into three of the four bowls on the table.

Miella and Kaia looked at the soup and then at each other, grimacing simultaneously. They knew full well that under normal circumstances neither of them would ever eat anything made in such shabby conditions, but they were ravenous and had no choice other than to eat it or starve.

Appie handed them the bowls. They watched in amazement as he picked his bowl up and drank from it as though he was drinking from a cup, slurping loudly to make matters even worse!

Miella and Kaia had dined in the company of many powerful and sometimes famous people who were their parents' friends or clients. For a few brief moments they were grateful their parents were not around to witness the table manners of this man. They would have been horrified.

Unsure of what to do, Kaia reluctantly decided to copy the old man. Miella soon followed.

The soup was the colour of muddy water, but despite its appearance, Miella thought it tasted rather good. Either that or she must have been so hungry that anything would have tasted good.

"I'm still hungry, what else have you got? But this time try and make it something that actually tastes good!" Kaia said rudely whilst pushing his empty bowl towards Appie.

Appie didn't respond.

"KAIA!" Miella exclaimed in disbelief, "Apologise NOW!"

"NO! Why should I? Anyway, it would be a waste of time, it's not like the dumb old man can understand."

"I'm sorry about him," Miella said to the bemused old man and thanked him for the food. She couldn't be bothered to deal with Kaia, she had more pressing matters on her mind, "Appie, we need your help."

The old man looked at her blankly.

"Our parents – you know... MUM... DAD... are lost. We need to find them... look for them," added Kaia, pointing at his eyes when saying the word *look* and speaking to the old man in such a condescending tone of voice that Miella could only hope he didn't understand. This may have been the case as he didn't respond.

Miella grew concerned as the lack of sunlight in the hut clearly indicated that it was getting dark outside. She had no idea as to how much time had passed since they had last seen their parents.

Suddenly remembering the picture of their parents, Miella spotted her bag lying on the floor by the bed she had been sleeping on and ran over to it. To her relief, the photo was still there and undamaged thanks to the fact that her bag was waterproof. She ran back over to the old man and showed him the photo.

"This is my mum, dad and Zophia," she said.

"And that's my mum and dad," said Kaia, kneeling up on his stool excitedly, "We need to find them!"

Appie said something in his language.

"Do you think he understands us?" Miella asked Kaia. Kaia looked at his cousin, he had no idea.

"Please try to understand. We need you to help us find these people!" Miella pleaded, pointing at the picture.

Appie smiled understandingly. He took the photo and placed it in the middle of the table,

"Sleep, bed, now," he said, pointing at their little beds.

"Morning," he then said, pointing at the picture.

The children, content knowing that he was willing to help, did as they were told and fell asleep hopeful of things turning out alright.

IV

The following morning, the children awoke to find some bananas and cracked coconuts for breakfast served on the table. here was no sign of the old man.

Miella looked around to see if she could find a clock or watch for the time, but there wasn't one to be seen. She also saw her bag on the table and whilst walking over to it, remembered the previous night's conversation. She hoped Appie's absence meant that he had already started the search. Kaia had now joined his cousin at the table and was chomping away on a banana.

She looked at him. His once beautiful and shiny golden brown curls were now horrible matted clumps. She tried to run her fingers through her hair but all she could feel were knots. She dreaded to think about the state she was in.

Looking around the room she thought about how much she had taken her life for granted. The very thought of living here forever made her shudder. She remembered Zophia always saying she and Kaia didn't appreciate what they had. That they were too spoilt and there would be a time when they would need to survive on their own and she was worried they would not be able to cope. Miella couldn't help but think there was now some truth to those words.

"Mimi, what are we going to do now?" Kaia asked, having finished his food.

"How am I supposed to know?" She snapped back.

Kaia looked slightly startled by her sharp response. "I'm sorry Kaia, I just really don't know what to do. I wish mum and dad were here." Miella started to cry. Kaia lent over and hugged her.

"Let's not hang around here getting upset. Let's go outside and explore. Who knows, we might find someone else to help us find them or perhaps even find them ourselves!"

Miella was quite surprised by Kaia's words and actions. He was usually such a pain and a complete nuisance, but this time he seemed genuine. And what he was saying not only comforted her, but made sense.

With Miella agreeing to his suggestion, Kaia didn't waste any time. He climbed up on a stool and lifted the hook off the door latch. He jumped off the stool and Miella moved it away. Grabbing the handle, he paused and looked at Miella,

"Ready?" he asked. She nodded.

As he pulled the wooden door towards him the bright light and intense heat hit them both. They stepped outside to a completely breath taking view. Their bare feet were touching the softest and golden sand they had ever felt and seen, the water in front of them was the clearest blue imaginable. Lined along the beach were palm and coconut trees.

Kaia started running towards the sea and dived in. Miella followed. The warm water touching their hot skins felt incredibly comforting.

They were a little disheartened to notice that there were no other huts or people around. But the paradise that surrounded them, briefly, helped to take their minds off the events of the past few days.

V

Arriving back at the hut Appie expected to find the children still in bed or at least having breakfast but they were nowhere to be seen. Their absence didn't concern him. He knew there was no way for them to leave the island. And if they were lost, he knew he could find them. He knew they were missing their parents and felt sorry for them but he also knew they had a greater purpose and would be fine.

Looking around the hut he saw Miella's bag on the table surrounded by the messy remainders of breakfast. He picked up the bag, placed it carefully on top of a little wooden cabinet and sighed. He had so much work to do in preparing the children and hoped he was up to the job. He suddenly realised he had forgotten to change back to the person the kids knew him as, the old man. A shiver ran down his spine at the thought of their reaction if they were to see him like this. It would ruin everything! Transforming himself quickly back to the old man, he pulled the photo out from the bag and muttered, "Zophia-Eliane, I hope you are right about these kids!"

VI

"Kaia, maybe we should head back to the hut. I'm sure Appie will be worried if he returns to find us missing," Miella said, as she lay on the sand, soaking up the warmth and comfort of the heat from the sun.

"Like I really care about what he thinks!"

"Kaia, don't be like that! He's the only chance we have of finding the others... he might even have some good news for us when we get back, but just don't get your hopes up too high!" Miella stood up and wiped the sand off the back of her thighs. She then held out her hand as a gesture to help Kaia get up.

He really didn't want to move but couldn't be bothered to start an argument so he held his hand out to her and she pulled him up.

The two of them made their way back in silence.

VII

Appie could clearly see the disheartened expressions on the children's faces as they drew closer to the hut. He knew they would, very soon, be put out of their misery.

Kaia walked straight past him without saying a word or even making eye contact.

"Hello Appie," Miella muttered. "I don't suppose you have any news about our parents or when and how we can go home?"

Appie shook his head.

Miella smiled faintly at him and followed Kaia into the hut.

Appie started to walk away from the hut, further on into the island, towards a creek and sat on a rock. Holding his stick out and waving it over the water directly in front of him he started

21

to mutter and mumble words under his breath. Steam rose from the water causing it to bubble. Small tiny little ones at first, but then they got bigger and bigger. Appie stood up, jumped straight into the water and vanished!

… … …

Ricon

Catching a quick glimpse of his reflection as the old man, Appie transformed back to his real identity. A fourteen-year-old with a dark caramel complexion, dark brown eyes and black hair.

Checking his uniform was on correctly, he felt really happy to be back. His creamy white trousers and matching v-neck top were extremely comfortable; they made him feel like he was in pyjamas all the time. As he turned his head around, he caught the sight of the tip of one of his wings and smiled.

"Well hello there, Appie! It's been a while. How are the potential recruits handling things?"

In front of Appie stood a smiling brown-haired, green-eyed girl who was also about fourteen years of age.

"Tilly, it's been really difficult to see those kids as upset as they are. That's why I am here. I really need to see Zophia."

"I'm sure she's here somewhere! You know Zophia, always running around. Let's go and see if we can find her, we'll try her office first."

They walked out of the room into a magnificent hallway. There were a few other people walking around them but no one looked older than sixteen. They were all dressed in the same uniform and proudly carrying their wings on their backs.

They continued walking towards some glass like steps. There were hundreds of steps in front of them and at times like this their wings became very useful as they floated above the steps.

Each floor was split up by thirty steps or so. They headed straight to the top, the tenth floor. In front of them were two large red doors, with gold handles and golden trimmings around the edges.

Tamsin, whom everyone called Tilly, placed her hand on a screen which was to the right of the door. An electric blue current appeared highlighting its outline.

As the grand doors opened up, a big smiled exploded on Appie's face at the sight of all the action taking place in the huge hall in front of them. They walked down three golden steps to a floor also made of a solid gold material and found themselves amongst groups of children working on various martial-arts type activities. They were all there to learn to protect and defend themselves from the evil Tyrians and learn more about their duties as Riconians.

Looking around and seeing all the action taking place made Appie really excited about what was in store for Kaia and Miella. He was especially eager to see how they would react when they discover the truth!

Despite having trained so many children, he enjoyed every challenge with each child and he never grew tired of being a mentor.

As soon as they had reached the opposite end of the hall, Tilly placed her hand on another screen for another set of doors to open. Security had to be tight in case they ever came under attack, especially as they were now entering Zophia's office.

In the room in front of them, sat behind virtual monitors were Candace and Harpz. Twin sisters who were two of the most respected Riconians. Both were highly regarded, renowned for their skills as fighters and joint second in charge after Zophia. Their main job was to protect Zophia but they were also in charge of security in Ricon.

They were both very pretty with beautiful, smooth and shiny ebony hair and glowing dark complexions.

"Look at who I've found," said Tilly.

"Ladies… looking good as always, it's been a while hasn't it? I know you've missed me like crazy!" Appie always liked to think of himself as a bit of a charmer. He too was very good looking and modesty was certainly not one of his strengths.

Harpz started laughing but Candace rolled her eyes towards the back of her head.

"Some things will never change will they Appie? How are the latest potential recruits?" Harpz asked.

"Ready! Well… that's what I think and why I'm here. I need to speak to Zophia to see if she agrees."

"Ok, give me a minute, I'll just go and see if Zophia is available," replied Candace.

She stood up and walked towards a transparent cubicle attached to one of the walls. Upon entering it she muttered something and a platform appeared from under her feet raising her up in the cubicle which led to Zophia's office.

Harpz looked at her screen, "Zophia is ready for you."

Appie walked towards the cubicle with his nerves getting the better of him. He had never been in Zophia's office before and wasn't too sure of what to expect!

Zophia was a Riconian Master and therefore had to be respected but she was also very approachable and definitely like a mother figure to all the Riconians.

Appie stood by the cubicle door waiting for Candace to come back down. She opened the door for him and the platform elevated them towards Zophia's office. The cubicle drew to a sudden halt in front of a plain black wall. Candace opened the door.

"Don't worry," she said giggling at the puzzled expression on his face. "Just place your right hand on the wall and you'll see what happens."

Appie did exactly as he was told and felt like a large vacuum was sucking him in through the wall.

Zophia's office was huge! All around her were large virtual screens and a large window behind her desk from which Appie could see the bright lights of the stars. Appie heard the familiar and warm voice of Zophia coming from the left of him. He turned to face her.

"How are you my dear and to what do I owe the pleasure of seeing you here in my office?" She hugged and kissed him on both cheeks.

Zophia was exactly as the children knew her, around fifty years of age, olive skin, dark-brown hair, short and slightly plump. However, her appearance was not one to be deceived by. She was an extremely strong woman both physically and mentally, who was greatly feared by the Tyrians. They knew if Zophia wasn't around then their job would be much easier and for that reason alone tight security around Zophia and the headquarters was needed. Still, in all the years of Zophia being a Riconian Master the Tyrians hadn't dared try to attack.

"Please, have a seat!" Zophia said pointing at a big red couch.

Appie sat down. Zophia placed herself next to him.

"Zophia, I know it's not really my place to say this but I think it's time the children were told the truth. They are understandably very sad!"

Zophia turned her head towards one of her large screens to look at images of the children who were fast asleep in the hut.

"Ah yes, Kaia and Miella! You say they are unhappy? Well we can't have that now, can we? Appie you know how essential it is for them to be ready to undergo training when we tell them. I know Miella will be fine but what do you honestly think about Kaia?"

"Kaia is a slight concern for me but I'm sure he'll do what ever his cousin does."

"That's fine then Appie. Return back and prepare them for my visit. I will follow shortly. Just make sure you wait for me before you tell them anything!"

Zophia stood up and walked to the large black door. Appie followed. She took hold of his hand and the two of them were sucked through to the other side. She opened the door of the cubicle and Appie entered. Zophia gave him a rather mischievous smile and shut the door.

Instead of going down, the cubicle started to rise up and gradually increase in speed. Appie closed his eyes. All of a sudden he felt the cubicle disappear and everything stop. He found himself back on the island standing right next to the creek and caught his reflection in the water. He was back to being the old man, even his walking stick was beside him.

"Thanks Zophia," he said laughing, and then turned to make his way back towards the hut.

… … …

Island

I

The noise from the door opening and closing woke Miella up and she was pleased to see that Appie had returned. She was also relieved to see that Kaia was still asleep. She knew he was getting really frustrated and while he slept, she didn't have to deal with him or make excuses for his behaviour!

Miella looked at the old man and thought he had a rather curious expression on his face as she watched him walk towards Kaia. He touched his shoulder and gently shook it to wake him up. Kaia opened his eyes, yawned and started to rub them.

"Ok kids! Time to wake up and follow me!"

Miella and Kaia's were dumbfounded!

"You can speak English?" Kaia asked, looking very surprised.

"I'm a very fast learner," replied Appie, laughing with a twinkle in his eyes.

Miella and Kaia looked at each other, confused and uncertain of how to react. Miella walked towards Appie who was now standing by the door. Kaia remained where he was.

"Well what are you waiting for? Come on! Get moving!" Appie commanded, in a jovial tone.

"Where are we going? Have you found our parents? Are they ok? If you haven't then I sure am not going anywhere with you! What's the point?" Kaia asked, folding his arms and sulking.

"No, I'm sorry. I have no news just yet of your parents and as for where we are going to... well it's a bit of an adventure, if you want to find out more you just have to come along or you can stay where you are and be moody, it's your choice," Appie replied calmly.

Kaia looked at Appie knowing the old man was right. He was intrigued and wanted to know exactly where they were off to. He had become incredibly bored of sitting around, doing absolutely nothing. But he didn't know how to react as he had become accustomed to people coaxing and making a fuss of him.

"Kaia come on…" Miella started to say, but Appie stopped her.

"No Miella, he needs to decide by himself – so Kaia are you coming or not?"

Kaia looked at both his cousin and Appie, grudgingly unfolded his arms and stood up. "Suppose I might as well, seeing as though there is nothing better to do!"

"Great then, let's go," replied Appie, sincerely.

They walked out of the hut together, Appie in front with Miella and Kaia following behind in complete silence. The children were busy trying to figure out where Appie was taking them and what he was up to especially as all they could see in front of them was sand, sea and a few tropical trees scattered around. There were so many questions they wanted to ask but were too nervous to do so.

After walking for about two hours the children began to tire and their pace slowed down. Noticing this, Appie decided to stop under a coconut tree. He was quite impressed as he thought at least one of them would have mentioned something or complained much earlier. He was pleased to see they had the stamina needed to be a fighter.

"Can't you at least tell us where are we going? I can't take much more of this walking," moaned Kaia.

Appie decided it was best to ignore him.

"Appie, I'm very thirsty," said Miella.

"Look around you Miella. Can you see anything drinkable?"

Miella looked around her. All she could see was sea water which she already knew would not be suitable for drinking, sand, the tree they were stood under and a few rocks.

"No!"

"Are you sure? Have a proper look around you."

Miella had another look around her, just to please the old man.

"No!" Miella snapped back, as her hunger and thirst were beginning to really affect her.

30

"Well, if that's the case then it looks like we might be here for a while!" Appie said as he lazily sat down on the sand under the shade.

"Listen to me you crazy old fool! I'm fed up of all of this! What are you playing at? Firstly, you act like you can't speak or understand English. Then you take us on a stupid long walk. And now you decide to start talking in riddles? My cousin is thirsty. So am I! So stop with this silly game of yours!" Kaia yelled.

"KAIA!" Miella shouted sounding completely fed up. She slumped down to the ground keeping her back against the tree.

Kaia was taken aback and speechless. He thought he was sticking up for her!

"Appie, please! I am tired and very thirsty. I really need something to drink."

Appie said nothing at first, then slowly and calmly responded, "What are you sitting under?"

"A tree," replied Miella.

"Yes but what type of tree is it?" Appie asked, looking towards the top.

"A COCONUT TREE!" They were so relieved.

"Ok, now we finally have a solution. But how are we going to get one of them? Oh and I'm sorry for shouting at you earlier," Kaia said, mumbling the second half of the sentence.

Appie was amused and pleasantly surprised by Kaia's attempt at an apology. He certainly wasn't expecting one, even if it was half-hearted!

"Well, I was going to make you climb up the tree to get one yourself and then watch you use the rocks to crack them open, as you were so rude! But since you have just apologised to me I'll make it easier."

Appie stood up and stared at the top of the tree. A coconut became loose and started to freefall towards the ground. He stared at it again and quickly managed to get it under control before it hit the ground. Using his eyes, he then directed it towards an awestruck Kaia, who instinctively reached his hands out to take hold of it. Appie then did the exact same thing again, but this time gave it to an equally surprised Miella.

"Wow! How did you do that?"

Appie smiled.

"Don't worry Kaia, you'll soon find out and be able to do a whole lot more," he said, as he used his powers to open the coconuts for the children to drink from.

"Wow! Can I try to do it now? I want to get a coconut down myself!"

"Not right now Kaia, we need to get back. So are you ready for the long walk back?"

"Yep – no problems, lets get going," replied a now highly charged and enthusiastic Kaia.

Appie and Miella looked at Kaia and started to laugh at his sudden change of personality.

"I'm sorry to disappoint you Kaia but we won't be walking all the way back."

"So how are we going to get back, fly?" Kaia asked sarcastically.

"No… we are not but I am," and just as Appie said that, he began the transformation to reveal his true identity.

The glow Miella saw on the first day at the hut reappeared as his walking stick disappeared into a tiny object in his hand. Next his hunched over body started to straighten up and all his wrinkled skin began smoothing itself out. Finally his wings appeared.

Miella and Kaia both stepped back with horrified and frightened looks on their faces. Kaia was the first to faint. Miella somehow managed to sit down on a rock before passing out.

Appie wasn't too sure of what their reactions would be, but he certainly wasn't anticipating the both of them dropping like flies. He wasn't too concerned. It made his job of returning them back to the hut much easier. Instead of flying there, he would just use his powers to get them back.

II

Opening his eyes to find the both of them still in the hut, Kaia wondered if he had been dreaming.

"Miella, wake up... wake up, what just happened?"

Miella turned around to face Kaia who had his back to the front door, but just as soon as she did, her jaw dropped and her eyes opened up wide in shock. He turned around hesitantly to see what had caused his cousin to react in such a way.

"ZOPHIA!" Kaia yelled.

By now, Miella had tears streaming down her face. He too, feeling relieved, started to cry as he thought Zophia being alive would mean their parents were as well.

"Zophia, what are you doing here? Are you ok? Are the others ok? Where are they? What is going on?"

"Kaia, one question at a time!" Zophia said laughing. She walked towards them with Appie following closely behind.

"You! So I wasn't dreaming? Who are you? Where are we?" Miella asked.

"Miella, Kaia, I'm just about to explain everything to you so please calm down and make yourselves comfortable. I want you both to listen to me first and then you may ask me any questions you may have after."

Miella stood up and placed herself next to Kaia. They were both sitting opposite Zophia, ashen-faced from the shock.

Zophia looked at them and smiled warmly.

"Firstly, I want to assure both of you that your parents are fine. They are not dead, in fact nothing has happened to them. Life continues as normal for them, except in their minds neither of you ever existed. I know this is difficult for you to do but as they have no knowledge of you please try not to feel too sad.

Miella, I know you have the photo taken before we set sail. Where is it?"

"I think I last left it on the table in my bag," Miella replied weakly.

"I know where it is. I'll get it," said Appie, jumping to get the bag and then handing it to Zophia.

"Take the photo out, both of you have a look and tell me what you see," Zophia said, passing it to Miella.

"We're not there anymore, we've disappeared, you as well!"

"Exactly! They have no knowledge of either of you and are happily continuing with their lives. Miella continue to keep that photo safe as it will come in handy one day."

Miella nodded and placed it carefully back into her bag.

"Now you know your parents are safe and well, I imagine you would like an explanation as to what is going on," Zophia said, whilst gently wiping the tears from Miella's face.

"Well… we are known as Riconian Warriors and that is what the both of you have been chosen to become. We are protectors of children on Earth."

"What are you… angels?" Kaia asked, looking at Appie's wings.

"No. We are not. We are here to stop an evil force called the Tyrians from creating chaos on Earth. You know how big Earth is and your solar system alone, well just try to imagine how big the whole universe is. It's impossible! We Riconians don't even know how big it really is.

We live on a planet called Ricon in what we know as outer space, but we are not aliens! We were all humans once upon a time. Everyone, myself included, was made a Riconian before the age of sixteen and we have all been in positions similar to the one you are in now.

The Tyrians live on another distant planet. Unfortunately we do not know much about them. All we know is that they are led by a very evil being called Master Tyler and their quest is turn good children on Earth evil, so they then join their army and help take over Earth. They target children as they are the easiest to corrupt and manipulate.

If the Tyrians are successful then these children will be irreversibly damaged by the time they are adults and will cause serious devastation and destruction on Earth. And as adults have more power than children the consequences of their actions will be much worse.

As soon as they have caused as much damage on Earth and to humans as they can, they then become Tyrians."

"Wow!" Miella exclaimed.

"None of this has anything to do with me, I don't want to be a stupid Riconian or whatever it is you call yourselves, saving or helping stupid children. I WANT TO GO HOME!" Kaia shouted, with tears streaming down his face.

"Kaia, raising your voice and demanding things won't get you very far anymore. I understand why you are upset and frustrated. This is a lot for you to take in and you are right, I can't make you do something you don't want to do. No one can! However I'll make a deal with you, with both of you. I want you to think carefully about everything I have told you. Think about how exciting and new it will all be and how lucky you are to have been chosen to have this opportunity. Take the chance to see what it is all about. If after completion of your training you don't want to continue then I promise you can go back to life, exactly as it was.

Talk about it together. Sleep on it tonight. And then tomorrow morning inform Appie of your decisions. But you have to really want to do this for yourself! If by tomorrow morning either one, or both of you, really does not want to continue, you will be returned to your families immediately.

I'm afraid I now have to leave. Appie is your mentor. It is his job to help you become a Riconian, should you want to."

Before the children could respond, Zophia got up, walked towards the door, turned around and waved goodbye. But instead of opening the door to leave the hut she placed her right hand into her pocket, took something out of it and disappeared.

"Wow, would we learn to do that?" Miella asked in amazement.

"Of course you would," laughed Appie. "It's been a long day and I'm sure you are both tired and hungry. How about we make things a little more interesting and luxurious than you are used to?"

Appie then reached into his pocket and pulled out a little red egg shaped and sized capsule.

"Come closer and have a look at this!"

Kaia and Miella walked towards it nervously.

"Hold it yourselves if you want, it won't hurt you!"

"No thank you," said Kaia, as he stubbornly turned away and sat on the bed opposite Appie and Miella pretending not to be interested.

"Eugh, it feels really soft and squishy. What is it?"

"What do you want it to be Miella? Does this look familiar?" Appie asked, transforming the capsule into the walking stick he had used when he appeared as an old man.

"How did you do that?" Kaia shouted out, then quickly covered his mouth with his hand, because he had forgotten he was supposed to be sulking. Appie and Miella over at Kaia and started to laugh.

"Kaia, why don't you just come over here and stop pretending that you are not interested?" Miella asked. Kaia looked at her. He was trying to prove a point but who he was trying to prove it to he really didn't know so he joined them.

Appie took the stick and handed it to Kaia. As soon as Kaia took hold of it, it transformed back into its original form.

"This little red object is called a creator, the reason being that it can create and turn into pretty much anything you want as well as enabling you to change your appearance. It is very powerful, therefore you need to learn how to use it properly and only with good reason."

"Can I have a go at changing it now?" Miella asked.

"You can try if you want, but don't get too upset if nothing happens. Think of what you would like the object to become."

"Can I really change it into anything?" A million and one possibilities entered her mind.

"Normally, yes, but as it's your first time and you are just experimenting with it, think of something small. Definitely not anything large or heavy!"

Miella took Appie's advice into consideration. The creator was still in Kaia's hand so she looked around the room for inspiration.

"What do I have to do for it to change shape?"

"Just concentrate and focus on changing it into that object."

36

"That's all?" She took it out of Kaia's hand.

"Yep, that's all," replied Appie.

Miella looked around the room. Something caught her attention. It was a spider's web and Kaia was terrified of spiders. Smiling, she looked at the creator and also at Kaia who was mesmerised by it in the palm of her hand. She then closed her eyes and tried to picture the spider in the palm of her hand.

"ARRGGGHH!" Kaia screamed.

"Did I really do it?" Miella asked in disbelief, and then laughed at the look of horror on Kaia's face.

"Turn it back! You know how much I hate spiders!"

Miella, still laughing at her cousin, looked over at Appie. It was obvious he wanted to laugh but was trying hard not to. Miella returned the creator back to its original shape and handed it back to Appie.

"Well I guess you think you are really funny! Don't worry I'll get you back," snapped Kaia.

"Oh Kaia, get over it! You've been a pain since we got here. This is a shock to me too but I'm not being rude to everyone like you!"

Kaia looked at his cousin. He thought it was so typical of her, bossy and trying to portray herself as little miss perfect. Part of him felt like starting a fight. In his mind he pictured his arm reaching for her hair. It would feel incredibly good to give it a massive tug! He was about to do it but stopped himself. Miella was right, he had been acting like a pain, but he wasn't really bothered. He was more interested by everything that was happening. And the more he thought about it, the more impressed and excited he became at the thought of becoming a Riconian.

Appie looked at Miella.

"Miella, I have to admit that what you did was pretty funny, however, there are certain rules we have to stick by when we use our powers. You will learn more later on if you decide to become a Riconian but one of them is that your powers cannot be used in a negative way towards any human or Riconian. They maybe used against a Tyrian but only in self-defence."

"Oh sorry Appie! It's just that… well the first thing that came to mind was the spider's web."

"No harm done. You didn't really hurt him, and you didn't know the rules. Just remember for the next time," Appie said, and then winked at Miella.

"Both of you have had a really long and hard day and I'm sure you must be hungry. I know I am! I think you deserve a feast along with a few luxuries."

Appie took the creator in his hand and closed his eyes. Kaia and Miella could not believe what they were seeing.

The room they were standing in started to change before them. The untreated wooden planks on the floor turned into marble, the walls which originally were logs of wood transformed into white walls with beautiful paintings hanging from them. The wooden-beamed ceiling with bits of straw poking through from the roof had now become a solid white ceiling, from which a magnificent crystal chandelier hung. Under it, the rickety old table they used to eat on was now a splendid dining table upon which a feast was laid out. They couldn't wait to tuck in!

"Well, what do you think?" Appie asked laughing, as he turned to see both Miella and Kaia's faces with their jaws wide open.

"I'll leave you to enjoy your food and then get some sleep. If you turn around you'll notice you now have somewhere much more comfortable to sleep on."

They both turned to see the hard little wooden beds they had been sleeping on were both now beautiful big beds with big fluffy pillows and covers. They could not believe the room had changed so much.

"Where are you going? Aren't you going to stay with us?" Kaia asked Appie

"No. You two have much to discuss! I'll be back in the morning to find out what you have decided." Appie said before disappearing out of the room.

"Wow, I want to be able to do that… that is so cool!" Kaia said, running towards the table where Miella was and had already started eating the ice-cream.

"Imagine what mum and dad would say if they could see us now," laughed Miella, as they attacked the food in a similar way to how pigs would eat at a trough.

"We would be in serious trouble if they could!" Kaia replied.

After about ten minutes of stuffing themselves with everything in sight, they headed over to the beds and lay down on them facing each other.

"Mimi, today has been crazy! What do you think about everything that has happened?"

"I really don't know Kaia! I haven't had much of a chance to think about it. We know Zophia and she's always been good to us. It was a shock finding out who she really is!"

"I know! That really freaked me out. What do you think we should do about joining them?"

"Like Zophia said, Kaia, you need to figure this one out for yourself. I mean think of all those special powers we could have. And to be able to do all of those things Appie does would be so cool."

"That's exactly what I keep thinking about. The way you turned that creator thing into a spider was awesome, even if it was a *spider!*" Kaia said giving his cousin a really evil look after saying the words spider.

"Oh get over it! If it was anyone else you would have laughed too, and you know it!"

"Whatever!" Kaia replied knowing Miella had a good point.

"The only thing is I'm not too sure how I'll be able to handle never seeing mum and dad again. I'm really going to miss them."

"Me too! I'm really not sure of what to do. This is such a hard decision to make, *really* hard! I just don't know!"

"Kaia, the best thing we can do now is to get some sleep. Maybe in the morning we'll have a better idea of what to do. It's been such a long day and I am exhausted."

"Ok, goodnight," replied Kaia, yawning as his eyes started to shut.

"Yeah goodnight," said Miella, with her eyes shut and a weak smile on her face.

III

"Good Morning! How did you sleep last night?" Appie enquired, entering the house to find both the children seated at the table.

"Not too bad considering all that has happened!" Miella replied.

"It *was* an awful lot for you to take in but Riconians need to be able to deal with all kinds of situations. Consider it a taste of what's to come! So have either of you made a decision?"

Miella and Kaia looked at each other apprehensively.

"One more thing before I get an answer. In order to become a Riconian you need to forget about the past. Forget what has happened, who you used to be and concentrate on your tasks... your mind needs to be clear of any distractions, especially in order to use the creator effectively."

Nothing but a deadly silence came from either of the children.

"I'm sorry," replied Miella suddenly. "I can't do it... I want to go home! I just want to be back with my parents."

Appie was unable to hide the disappointment from his face. Kaia looked at his cousin who now had tears rolling down her cheeks. He too started to cry.

"I guess you feel the same way?" Appie asked Kaia.

"Well actually... no," he replied, trying to compose himself. "I want to give it a try. I want to become a Riconian. I have nothing to lose if I try it and if I don't like it then I can always go back... right?"

Miella and Appie both had looks of surprise on their faces. They automatically assumed he would do the same as Miella.

"Right... Well I must say I am very impressed Kaia. I didn't expect that to be your answer, are you sure about this?"

"Yes Appie... very sure!"

"Ok! I'll give you a few minutes to say your goodbyes. Miella if you then come over to me, I'll send you home."

"Kaia are you sure about this?"

"Yes! I was thinking about this last night and the way I see it is that it will all be an adventure. I want to give it a chance. Mum and Dad won't miss me… in their minds I never existed. The hardest part now is saying goodbye to you Miella!"

Miella gave him a hug and the two of them stood tearfully holding each other.

"It's best you get going now Miella," Appie said holding his hand out for Miella to take hold of it.

Miella stepped back and gently pushed Kaia away as she reached out to Appie.

"NO WAIT! I don't want to go back. If Kaia can do this then so can I! Everything you have just said makes sense. I want to give it a try too."

Kaia wiped the tears from his eyes and was left with a big smile on his face.

"Are you sure Miella? You know that by making this decision you'll have to stick with it until you complete your training. It's not going to be easy and there'll be no going back until the end."

"I know Appie… I'm ready!" Miella replied.

"Ok then great! Let's not waste any more time. Let's get going!" Appie said placing an arm over each of their shoulders. The three of them disappeared out of the room and off the island.

… … …

Ricon

I

"Welcome to Ricon!" Just as Appie had said that, Tilly walked into the room and introduced herself.

Kaia and Miella couldn't help but stare at Tilly. She was a pretty girl with long brown hair which in a striking way complimented her porcelain skin and big green eyes.

After a brief introduction, Tilly led them along the corridor and into the main hall way.

Kaia and Miella were so taken in by their new environment, they didn't pay much attention to what Appie and Tilly were saying. They all walked up the first flight of steps of the main staircase then turned right.

Laid out in front of them was a thick and deep red carpet with heavy, antique looking wooden doors concealing a number of rooms along a corridor. Next to each door was the screen which required a hand-print for it to open.

As they walked towards the room they were heading to, Kaia was mesmerised by Appie and Tilly's uniform, especially their wings. They looked like they were made of thin panels of glass but he could tell it wasn't exactly glass. Kaia couldn't quite figure out what the material was so he reached out to feel it. Miella saw what he was about to do and quickly pulled his hand back.

"Stop it," she mouthed at him.

He just looked at her and grinned cheekily.

They stopped in front of the third door along the corridor.

Appie placed his hand on the screen and the door slid open. The room they were looking at was amazing. It looked like a huge theatre with a stage at the front, beautiful drawings on the high ceiling and about three hundred seats made of blue velvet with gold trimming around the edges.

"This is the Ceremony Room. It is in this room that you will finally become a Riconian having completed your training," Tilly explained.

They all walked towards the front of the stage and as they got closer Miella spotted the backs of four heads in the front row.

Appie caught Miella's gaze.

"They are other children who are in exactly the same situation as you and have also only just arrived here."

At the bottom of the stage Miella noticed another two Riconians seated on the floor in front of the children. As soon as they saw Appie and Tilly approach them, they stood up to greet them.

One was male and the other was female. The male Riconian looked as though he was about thirteen-years-old. He had short black hair, hazel eyes and a sun-kissed complexion. The female Riconian was a sweet looking girl of a South American background. She had straight, jet black hair with a fringe swept to the side and stricking eyes which were almost as dark as her hair.

After the four Riconians had greeted each other, Appie told Kaia and Miella to take a seat in the front row next to the other children.

Appie, Tilly and the other two Riconians then stood at the base of the stage facing all the children.

Tilly took a step towards the children and started to speak, "I'd like to start by welcoming all of you to Ricon. You've all met me but let me introduce my fellow Riconians here with me... Christopher, Tania and Appie. They will also be assisting with your training.

The room we are in is called the Ceremony Room. Look around this magnificent place and imagine all the seats filled up with Riconians congratulating you on completion of your training. It's an amazing feeling, one you'll never forget.

Ricon as you may or may not know is a very small planet probably the same size as Europe. We are not in the same solar system as Earth but have many stars surrounding our planet, providing us with energy, light, oxygen and water.

Apart from some of your training you won't spend much time here on Ricon unless you later decide you wish to become mentors or be a part of base security.

The six of you will be training together. Christopher is the person we need to thank for bringing Ilene and Conor to Ricon," as Tilly said that, she pointed to the two kids furthest away from Miella and Kaia.

They both leaned forward twisting their heads to get a better look. Ilene had an olive complexion with curly black hair and dark eyes. Conor had blond/brown hair, sparkling blue eyes and looked like a giant as his head towered above the other children.

Tilly continued, "The next two who were brought here by Tania, are Prashan and Patricia".

Miella was seated next to Patricia, she didn't want to stare at her in case she appeared rude, all she could see was very blond hair. Prashan seemed tiny sat next to Conor but in reality he was about the same height as Kaia which was just above average for a twelve-year-old. He had dark brown hair and a very unique look about him.

Tilly then briefly introduced Kaia and Miella to the other children.

"There's not much point in wasting time with longer introductions as you'll have plenty of time during training to get to know each other. Are there any questions so far?" Tilly asked.

Prashan meekly raised his arm in the air,

"How long does training usually last and what do we have to do?"

"Good question! I'll leave that to Christopher to answer."

"Thanks Tilly!" Christopher replied sarcastically, having been caught off guard.

"Hello everyone, I hope all this information isn't too daunting. There is no set time scale for training as such. Groups have taken anything from one month to about eight months in which to pass.

Training itself is based around this little object... the creator. You all know what this is and what it can do. When you have mastered using it and we feel you are confident and competent at using it, you'll then have to successfully accomplish your first assignment on Earth in order to complete your training. That's about it really, is there anything else anyone would like to ask?"

There was no response.

"Great! Well in that case I believe Tania has something she would like to give all of you."

Tania stepped forward, "Indeed I do. I have six brand new creators along with their own special pouches for you to keep them safe in until you get used to them. Before I hand them out, I have a question."

Tania pulled one of the creators out of its pouch and also her own. She held them both in the air, "I have an easy enough question, what's the difference between these?"

"One's yellow and the other's red," replied Ilene nonchalantly.

Slouching in his seat, Kaia thought it was so obvious an answer it had to be wrong, and smiled smugly whilst thinking about how stupid she would look for saying so.

"Correct!" Tania replied.

Kaia raised an eyebrow in disbelief at the stupid question, but it caught his attention so he sat up straight and started to take in what was being said.

"There's a reason for this. A yellow creator is a weak one. You need to have the right attitude and be strong in mind to control its power. It will keep changing colour throughout the first part of your training, gaining more power until it finally reaches red. That's when it is at its strongest.

Please look after these very carefully as you'll only ever get one. They will never break so the only way of you being parted from one is if you lose it."

Tania then handed one to each child.

Appie stepped forward and started to speak.

"That's all to be mentioned for now. The next thing to do is to show you all your rooms and you can spend sometime getting to know each other. Follow me!"

Appie then walked up the steps towards the door at the top with all the children closely behind him and the other three mentors following behind the children.

They walked back along the corridor to the main set of steps, then up the next two flights of steps to the third floor and turned left.

This corridor was different to the others. It had a more modern and futuristic feel to it with white walls and mirrored doors. Appie stopped at the first door as the others gathered behind.

"Are you all ready to see your room?"

He opened the door.

The children entered the room and the expressions on their faces changed from excitement to immense disappointment. The room was empty, there wasn't even any paint on the walls.

Appie looked over at Tania, Christopher and Tilly. They were all standing by the entrance with big grins on their faces. Tilly gently shook her head from side to side trying to conceal her laughter by covering her mouth.

"Well, what are we supposed to do here? Where are we going to sleep? There aren't even any beds for us! This is horrible!" Ilene shrieked out aloud in disgust.

Miella looked at Ilene. It was exactly what she was thinking but didn't dare say so. She thought the two of them would probably get along quite well.

"I get it," laughed Conor. "This is some kind of test, isn't it? We're supposed to use our creators to transform the room, right?"

"Wrong!" laughed Appie

"But that's actually a very good idea! I should think about doing that to our next set of recruits. But it's not what I have in mind for you. What I want all of you to do is stand together in a circle, hold hands and close your eyes."

They all looked at him dubiously until Miella took hold of Kaia's hand and as Patricia was standing next to her, reached out for hers. The others soon joined in. Appie held on to the creator in his right hand and placed his left hand on Patricia's shoulder as she was directly in front of him. All of a sudden the children disappeared.

Tania turned to Christopher and Tilly, "Honestly! What are we going to do with Appie? Always the joker! Ricon would not be the same without him," laughed Tania.

"Did you see the looks on their faces? Too funny... the whole thing was just too funny," added Christopher, as he shut the door behind him. They walked along the corridor back towards the main staircase and flew all the way up to the second to last floor. They then turned left.

In front of them this time was what looked like a large mirror. Tilly placed both her hands on it. A bright neon blue light travelled down from the top of the mirror, scanning them. The mirror then disappeared to reveal another room which they entered.

The room was huge. In one corner were four very comfortable looking beds and on the opposite corner was a door which led to the bathroom. In the centre was a huge square sofa facing a wall on which hung a huge flat screen television.

"Right! They should all be there now, let's see how they are doing," said Tania as an image came on the screen.

… … …

Island

Kaia, Patricia, Conor and Prashan found themselves either on their bottoms or face down in the sand. Somehow Miella and Ilene landed on their feet.

"Not exactly the smoothest of landings. I'm sorry," Appie said chuckling at the sight of all the different positions the children had ended up in.

"I'm back on the island!" Patricia exclaimed as she stood up and wiped the sand off the back of her blue jeans.

"Yes, you are back! In fact all of you have spent time here but on different parts. If anyone is wondering, you are all back on Earth but this island has and never will be detected by any human as there is a shield which makes it invisible. Now if you all follow me, I'll show you to your real new home," he said, walking away from the ocean and towards a part of the island which looked like they were heading into a jungle. Having walked for about ten minutes another little wooden hut with a roof thatched from various types of leaves came into view.

"Welcome to your new home!" Appie said, as he stopped in front of the door, waiting for everyone to gather around him. Trailing right at the very back was Prashan, both he and Patricia seemed to be the quietest and shyest of the group.

"Before we enter I should warn all of you that the inside is quite sparse but the sooner your creators become stronger, the sooner you can make it look the way you want."

Appie opened the door and they all walked in.

"Boy-oh-boy! You really were not joking when you said it was quite empty inside," Ilene said, in a very flat and unimpressed tone.

The main room contained just a dining table and six chairs. The floor was made of very old wooden blocks and the only light in the room came from two candles burning in their holders on the centre of the table.

Appie picked up one of the candles and walked towards a door positioned at the back of the room.

"This will be your bedroom," he said, opening the door to reveal six made up single beds in two rows of three facing each other and absolutely nothing else in the room.

"The door at the opposite end of the room leads to the bathroom."

Kaia and Miella looked at each other with the same disgusted expressions on their faces. They were used to living in luxury and having '*only the best that money can buy*', well that was what Miella's mother always used to say to her. This was to be a whole new way of living for them and one they were not happy about.

Appie then turned around and walked back through the main room towards another door on the other side, opposite the bedroom, and called the children over. As soon as they had gathered around him he placed his hand on the handle of the door.

"Ok get ready for your top of the range kitchen… you have no idea how lucky you all are!"

He pushed the door open and all of their eyes opened wide and jaws dropped.

"This is some kind of wind up, right?" Kaia asked Appie.

"It's just a rusty tap in an empty room!" Conor added.

"Appie if this is another of your so-called jokes well then stop now because it isn't funny. There is no way I am going to accept *that* as a kitchen!" stated a very angry Ilene.

"Well you'll have to! Like I said earlier, it's up to all of you to make something of it," replied Appie.

"Oh let me guess, the bathroom is in the same condition!" Ilene stated dismissively.

"No, no," laughed Appie

"Now, *that* I wouldn't do to any of you! There's a shower, sink and toilet in there."

"How… very… kind… of… you," Ilene replied in a slow, disrespectful tone as she stomped over to the table, pulled a chair out and sat on it in the most temperamental manner with her back facing everyone.

"Ilene looks rather lonely at the table, let's join her," suggested Appie, completely unfazed by her behaviour, as he had dealt with children much worse.

Miella on the other hand was shocked by what she was seeing. She wasn't happy about the situation either but couldn't believe the way Ilene was acting.

Appie walked over to the table and using the creator added an extra chair and sat down on it. The others followed in silence and joined him at the table. Ilene placed both her elbows up on the table, put her head in her hands and looked down in an attempt to ignore them all.

"Appie, can I ask you a question?" Patricia asked, trying to lighten the uncomfortable atmosphere in the room.

"Sure you can!"

"How is it that Zophia is a Riconian but is so old compared to everyone else?"

"Phew, I thought you were going to ask me something much more difficult, like maybe a maths question," he chuckled, trying to ease the tension.

"Zophia was chosen to be Head of Ricon by a group of individuals we called the Higher Beings. They rarely ever communicate with anyone except her. They are also the ones to decide who gets chosen to become a Riconian, and give us the subjects of our assignments.

As soon as you become the Head of Ricon you start to age naturally so when you die another Riconian can then take over. No Riconian has ever died or been injured permanently as we have the ability to heal ourselves using the creator... a Riconian may also heal the subjects of your assignments but cannot stop them from dying or help to heal any non-subject.

From the moment you become a Riconian you stop aging physically. As our subjects are young children it makes sense to remain young in appearance, however our minds age as they naturally would.

I might look like a fourteen-year-old but I'm really twenty-six-years-old and have been a Riconian now for twelve years. Tania, Christopher and Tilly are also much older than they appear to be. Zophia has lived on Ricon for over forty years.

Harpz and Candace, the two sisters who guard her, are probably in their mid-thirties."

"So who's going to be the next Head of Ricon?"

"Candace or Harpz or even perhaps the both of them. It entirely depends on what the Higher Beings decide... unless you show them you can do a better job Kaia!" Appie joked.

"Somehow I don't think that is going to happen anytime soon!" Kaia replied.

"Perhaps we are getting slightly ahead of ourselves, but stranger things have happened, so who knows!" Appie replied with a cheeky grin.

"I now have to return to Ricon. Take the rest of the evening as an opportunity to get to know each other a bit better. Are there anymore questions before I leave?"

Prashan raised his hand up slightly.

"Appie, we need clothes, toothbrushes and toothpaste... where can we get those? I can't sleep unless I brush my teeth," he said meekly.

Kaia looked at Prashan in disbelief, and Ilene snorted in an attempt to stop herself from bursting into fits of laughter. Appie shot the two of them a look of disapproval for their behaviour.

Kaia had already thought Prashan was a bit strange, but now, he was certain he was a complete nerd.

"Normally you'd have to learn to get those things with the creator but as I'm in a good mood today, you'll find these items on the beds.

You will be living here on the island on your own but we'll be observing all of you constantly. Remember you are here to be tested, so good luck!" Appie said, and then disappeared along with the extra chair he had been using. Upon his departure appeared some food and six bottles of water.

II

"So are you brother and sister?" Conor asked Kaia and Miella attempting to start up a conversation.

"No... cousins actually," Miella said.

53

"I don't mean to appear rude but I'm very tired so I think I just might go to bed now. Does anyone mind which bed I sleep in?" Prashan asked quietly and very politely.

"No, you choose whichever you want and we'll try not to disturb you when we come in," replied Patricia, smiling kindly at him.

"Ok then goodnight everyone," Prashan said, and walked into the bedroom.

"Is it me or does anyone else here think he is a total freak?" Kaia asked after the door had shut.

"I totally agree with you! He is such a weirdo," replied Ilene, laughing along with Kaia.

Miella, Patricia and Conor just sat silently whilst Kaia and Ilene continued to joke and laugh at Prashan's expense.

"You shouldn't be so judgemental, give him a chance!" Miella said.

"Oh please Mimi! Did you not hear what he said… I really can't sleep unless I brush my teeth," Kaia repeated, mimicking Prashan, "What an idiot!"

"THE ONLY IDIOTS AROUND HERE ARE YOU TWO!" Patricia yelled, "I would much rather be in a room with Prashan than stuck here listening to this," she continued with her voice still full of fury but not as loud in case Prashan overheard.

"If you want to prove how cool you are then try picking on me," she said standing up suddenly whilst glaring hard at Kaia and Ilene. "Well… what are you waiting for," she continued.

"No, I really didn't think either of you had it in you. You're both pathetic. I'm outta here," she said, grabbing a bottle of water and storming out of the main room into the bedroom.

"What's her problem?" Ilene asked rhetorically.

Miella, Kaia and Conor sat around the table in silence.

"I'm pretty tired too so I think I'll also get some sleep. It was good meeting you all today. I'll see you in the morning," Conor said after a couple of uncomfortably silent seconds. He then got up and walked out of the room.

"So what's the deal with you two? How did you end up on this island with me and the freaks?" Ilene asked.

Miella's initial opinion of Ilene had changed drastically and she wasn't keen on her at all now. Kaia however was glad Ilene was there. He thought they were very similar in personality and decided to be the one to tell her their story.

"So for at least a couple of days you both thought your parents were dead. That's so wrong, they shouldn't have done that!" Ilene remarked.

"Well actually, they never said anything about our parents. We thought the worst and got upset by ourselves for no reason. I guess that was a good lesson to learn, not to expect the worse all the time."

As soon as Miella had said that, she felt a tingle in her pocket. It was coming from the creator. She pulled it out of the pouch. It had changed colour from yellow to green.

"Wow, how did that happen?" Kaia asked, feeling slightly jealous.

"I don't know!" Miella replied starring in amazement at the creator.

Kaia immediately pulled out his creator, looked at it and said, "It's a good thing not to expect the worse all the time... Nothing is happening," he said to the other two in disappointment.

They both looked at each other and laughed.

"Oh Kaia! Sometimes I just don't know what to do with you," Miella said as she put the creator back in her pocket.

"Kaia, somehow, I doubt it would be that easy to make it change colour," Ilene said, still smiling.

"By the way, where are you from?"

"We're from London, our mums are English but our dads' parents are from different countries." Miella replied.

"London! I love it there, it's a pretty cool city but it rains quite a bit too. Do you miss your folks and home?"

"I haven't had the chance to miss them to be quite honest, well maybe the luxuries. Our parents are quite wealthy so this is very different to what we are used to. I honestly don't know how I'm feeling at the moment. How about you Kaia?"

Kaia, still engrossed by his creator, hadn't been paying attention to what the girls were talking about. "Eh? Did you just ask me something?" He noticed they were both looking at him in a way that required some kind of reaction.

"Never mind!" Miella said, rolling her eyes up towards the sky.

"So, what about you? What's your story? Do you miss your family?" Miella asked Ilene

"Well where do I start? My mother is from the Middle East and my father is Australian. They are a little like your parents except they both have successful careers as lawyers. They met when mother went to Australia to study law and as they both dealt in International Law we travelled around the world a lot. I've never really been in one place long enough to make any real friends and as for missing them… NO WAY!

My father recently moved out to live with his secretary and that drove mother crazier and turned her into a bigger pain than she already was! Not too long after my father left she made friends with this old woman, no prizes for guessing who! Zophia then introduced me to her 'grandson' Christopher who was about my age.

After a few of months, Zophia told mother that she wanted to take me on holiday with Christopher, so he could visit his parents who lived on an island they owned. Initially mother wanted to join us but Zophia managed to persuade her against that idea. Cutting a long story short when we arrived here Christopher told me who he really was, showed me some tricks with the creator, and here I am!

As for missing my parents… my father was never around much. And mother always thought of me as an extra hassle she never had the time for, so we are both much better off without each other. Well that's the way I see it!"

"I'm sorry to hear that," Miella replied.

"Don't be, I'm not. Anyway bad stuff happens to everyone its how you deal with it that matters. I just put the past in the past and concentrate on what is happening at present. Right now, that is doing whatever it takes to become a Riconian.

Anyway I'm tired now so I'm going to try and get some sleep... hold on... something's just happened!"

Ilene pulled out her creator. It too had turned green.

"Oh that is really unfair! I bet that just happened because of all that deep stuff you just said." Kaia mumbled unhappily.

"Don't worry! I'm sure you'll be next," Ilene said, trying to make him feel better.

They all then decided to get some sleep. Entering the bedroom, they saw that the three beds on one side of the room had been taken up by Conor, Patricia and Prashan. On the other beds opposite were all the things Appie had said he would leave out for them to use.

They wished each other a good night and went about getting ready for bed.

III

"ARGHHHH! I need to wash my hair and we have no water at all!"

Miella was woken up suddenly by Ilene's loud screechy voice.

She sat up and tried to pay attention. Kaia and Conor were still asleep and there was no sign of Patricia and Prashan

"What's wrong?" Miella asked.

"There's no running water, that's what is wrong! Only the toilet flushes and I'm not going to stick my head down there!"

"Oh that's a shame, I'd have liked to have seen that," said Patricia, as she entered the room with Prashan to see what all commotion was about.

"I'm not in the mood for your stupid comments!" Ilene replied sharply.

"Oh yeah is that a fact? So what are you gonna do about it?" Patricia asked aggressively.

"Ok, that's enough! It's far too early to start fighting! Let me try and sort out the problem," said Conor, jumping out of bed and walking to the bathroom.

Patricia shot Ilene a dirty look before following him.

"Kaia wake up. We could do with your help, we have a little situation here," Miella said.

"I know! Do you think I'm able to sleep with all the noise coming from those two?" Kaia replied with his eyes still shut. "I'll help out later. I'm tired," he continued.

"We need your help now," Miella insisted.

"It's ok, I'll help! Let me go and check the tap in the kitchen," offered Prashan.

"Good idea! I'll come with you, perhaps the problem's there," added Conor.

"This is really strange as everything was working fine earlier on." Prashan commented, as they walked out of the room.

"See, the nerd is helping out! There's no need for me now, is there?" Kaia mumbled to Miella.

"*I'll* go and see if there is anything I can do!" Miella said coldly as she headed towards the door.

She suddenly turned around, walked back to her bed full of rage, picked up her pillow, aimed it at Kaia's head and threw it hard at him.

"OUCH! What was that for?" Kaia yelled as he turned around to see who had thrown the pillow at him. "Miella!"

She ignored him and with a satisfied grin on her face walked out of the room.

"Oh well, seeing as though everyone is busy trying to sort the water out, I might as well get back in bed. What else is there to do around this dump?" Ilene moaned pointlessly to Kaia, as he huddled back under the covers, trying to get back to sleep, and paying her no attention.

Meanwhile, in the kitchen, Miella, Conor and Prashan were fiddling about with the tap trying to get some water running from it. Patricia walked into the room and stood by the doorway silently watching the others.

"It's no use! I think Appie left the bottles of water last night because he knew this would happen today," Miella said out aloud.

"You all really make me want to laugh! Hasn't it occurred to any of you that this is one of their tests and we should try to use the creator?" Patricia asked.

"Of course! Now all this makes sense. How do I do this again? Close my eyes and imagine water running out of the tap whilst holding it, right?" Conor asked the others.

"I guess that's how you would do it. That's how I managed to make it work for me," Miella replied.

"Ok… here goes…" Conor said as he held onto his creator, and closed his eyes.

"Any luck?" He asked after a couple of seconds, peaking through one eye.

"Nope," replied Miella.

"Ok, let's have another go at this," he said trying a second time.

"Still no luck, I'm sorry to say… maybe we should try together as ours are not very powerful on their own just yet," suggested Prashan

"That's a good idea. Should I go and get Kaia and Ilene?" Miella asked.

"Perhaps the four of us should have a go together first and if that doesn't work, we can get the other two," Patricia said walking towards the tap.

The four of them placed one hand on the tap and held on to their creators with the other.

At first a little trickle of water came out but after a few seconds a gurgling sound came from the tap and the water poured out, splashing them in the process. They were ecstatic.

"Wow! Look my creator has turned green!" Prashan exclaimed excitedly.

"Mine too," added Conor.

Miella saw hers had now changed from green to blue. She noticed Patricia putting hers away in its pouch really quickly. It was also blue.

"Patricia, I think both of ours are the same colour!"

"Really?" Patricia replied sounding very relieved.

"After the incident last night mine turned green. I thought I had done something awful," she said quietly so Prashan would not hear and question her about the 'incident'.

"No, I think it just means ours are getting closer to turning red," replied Miella.

"I'll check to see if the water is running in the bathroom and then let Kaia and Ilene know we've fixed it," said Conor, unaware that he was interrupting their conversation.

"I have to get dressed so I'll come along with you. What are you two going to do?" Miella asked Prashan and Patricia.

"I think I might just head down to the beach and sit there for a while," Patricia replied.

"Would you mind if I joined you?" Prashan asked.

"Of course not, it would be nice to have some company."

"Sounds like a good idea, I'll join you both after I get ready," added Miella.

"Cool, see you then," replied Patricia as they walked out of the front door and into the sunshine.

IV

As soon as Miella left the house, she realised she couldn't quite remember her way back to the beach. All she could recollect was the little path they had walked on for some of the way. She turned around to have a good look at the hut in daylight and shook her head in disbelief. She had never imagined there ever being a reason for her to live in such a place. It looked much smaller from the outside than she remembered and in a strange way it also looked much nicer than when she had first seen it.

There were some pretty plants around it and one in particular grabbed her attention as she had never seen anything like it before. Instead of the leaves being green they were bright blue and at the top were a couple of pink flowers growing out of them.

She decided to risk getting lost by trying to find Patricia and Prashan as she thought it would be a good way to familiarise herself with the island. Whilst walking she kept looking out

60

for more of the blue plants that she saw by the cottage but unfortunately she didn't come across any.

She smiled as she noticed the ocean from a gap in between some of the tropical palm trees and plants. The closer she got to the gap the more audible the sounds of the waves from the ocean became. She walked through, onto the sand and saw two small figures sitting by the sea.

"That was nice and easy," she muttered, as she walked over to Patricia and Prashan.

"So what have you two been up to?"

"Nothing much, just enjoying the sun and the view. It's so beautiful here. I'd never seen sights like this until Tania brought me here," Prashan replied.

"I feel as though I owe you both an apology for Kaia's behaviour last night," Miella said.

"I don't see why you have to apologise for your cousin's behaviour, but I'm also sorry for going off like that. I just really hate to see people acting the way he and Ilene did last night," Patricia replied.

"What happened last night? Did I miss out on something?" Prashan asked.

"No, it was just little disagreement," Patricia replied.

"Oh I'm glad I wasn't there, in that case. I hate it when people get into arguments. And I especially hate seeing people fight," Prashan replied.

"Like I said, I'm sorry," replied Miella, taking note of how sensitive Prashan was. "So what were you talking about?" Miella asked, wanting to change the subject.

"Just how we ended up here, what's your story?" Prashan enquired.

Miella repeated the story whilst Prashan and Patricia listened attentively.

"Oh well, at least you have the chance to go back to your parents at the end." Prashan said after hearing Miella's story.

"Why can't you do the same?" Miella asked, finding it difficult to believe he wasn't given the same option.

"No, no I can go back to my old life but my Mum is dead and I never knew my dad."

"Oh! Sorry to hear that!" Miella replied.

"It's a complicated story!"

"I've got time to listen and I *love* stories," Miella said, with a cheeky smile on her face.

"Well if you really want to know then sure, I'll tell you," answered Prashan, slightly confused as to why Miella was so interested.

"My parents were from very strict families. My dad's family is Indian and my mum's were Chinese. My mum fell pregnant with me when she was seventeen and had to tell her parents. They were furious and kicked her out of the house. My dad's parents took the news so badly they moved away and my mum never found out where they went. I'm named after my dad, although I guess I look a lot more like my mum.

She was great... the best! She did her best bringing me up on her own. We never had much and lived on a rough estate but I remember always being happy when she was alive.

She died when I was ten-years-old. She was knocked down by a car on her way home from work one evening. The police never found out who did it because the driver never stopped."

"Oh I'm sorry to hear that," replied Miella, wishing she had never asked in the first place. "Is that how you ended up here?"

"Not straight away! I was put in a children's home and it was not nice. Fights were breaking out all the time and there was one boy in particular who always started trouble. I tried to keep to myself and found the best way to do that was to create a routine and try to stick to it."

Miella then remembered Prashan's comment about brushing his teeth the night before and it all started to make sense.

"One day that boy tried to start a fight with me but I got the better of him and he ended up in hospital for months. There was talk of me being sent to a children's prison. I had never been in a fight before and felt awful after!

I had to have a lawyer represent me in court and guess who that was... yes Zophia! Somehow, she managed to get me out of going to prison, and then told me about Ricon and who she really was. She also told me a little secret I am never allowed

62

to repeat about my mum, it helped me deal with her death a lot better.

I then met Tania who brought me to the island. The two of us had so much fun just relaxing and playing games. I can't wait to become a Riconian now!" Prashan said smiling.

Miella didn't know what to say, she had never heard of or known anyone who had been through as much as him. Luckily Patricia broke the silence. "I guess being here is exciting, but I can't help but think about my family back home!"

Miella wanted to ask her about her family but wasn't in the mood to hear another depressing tale. But curiosity got the better of her and Miella just had to know, "Ok, I admit it! I'm nosey, what's your story?"

"It's one that is too long to tell right now, especially as I can see the others walking towards us," replied Patricia.

"We're all hungry and tried to use the creator to get some breakfast but the stupid thing wouldn't work. I think we need to use them together. Just like how you guys did this morning," Ilene said as she stood over the three of them who were still seated on the sand.

"Should we go back to the hut?" Miella asked.

"I think we should have breakfast out here. Look at how beautiful it is!" Conor said.

"Fine, let's stay here but how do we do this?" Kaia asked, having never used his creator before.

"We all need to think about what we want and then imagine it in front of us," said Prashan.

"Well, I want a big piece of chocolate cake, no in fact a whole cake all to myself!" Kaia pulled out his yellow creator and closed his eyes as he imagined it in front of him. Nothing happened.

"Why is this stupid thing not working?" Kaia moaned.

"Maybe it's because yours is still yellow and ours have turned green. Let me try, and if it works then I'll eat it all myself and make you watch me eat every last crumb!" Ilene said half jokingly.

Again nothing happened.

"Why isn't mine working now?" Ilene asked frustratedly.

"Maybe it's because the two of you are being greedy. Let me see if I can make one that we can all share."

Miella pulled her creator out of her bag where she kept her photo and took it out of its pouch.

"Miella, why has yours turned blue?" Kaia asked

"Because I helped to get the tap working while your lazy backside was still in bed," she snapped, before imagining a cake large enough for all of them to share. As soon as she did one appeared on her lap.

"Yum! That looks really good! How about I try to get a blanket, some plates, drinks and glasses so we can have a picnic breakfast?" Kaia offered, knowing from the way Miella had just spoken that she was mad at him. He thought he had better try and do something nice, kind of like a peace offering, otherwise Miella would just hold her grudge for longer.

He held on tight to his creator and concentrated really hard. A red and white checked picnic blanket appeared about half a meter from where they were all gathered. On top of it appeared some plates, cutlery, glasses, juice and some water. Right next to Miella a single yellow rose appeared.

Kaia opened his eyes, looked at her and said, "I'm sorry!"

Miella simply smiled at him.

Kaia looked at his creator it had turned blue straight away he was happy that it was no longer yellow but couldn't work out why it had jumped to blue instead of first turning green. He just put it down to the fact that he had just done two different things. Sorted out the picnic stuff and apologised to Miella. Miella's had now turned purple.

The others then thought of food and as they did all of their creators changed to the next colour. Only Patricia and Miella had purple creators, the others were now blue. They all sat around and had their breakfast.

"Is it me or is the sun starting to get really hot? I can feel my skin burn and I'm getting very hot out here." Conor said, after they had finished eating.

"I was starting to think that too!" Miella admitted. Some of the others nodded their heads in agreement.

"Maybe we should make our way back to the hut as it was much cooler in there?" Prashan suggested.

"Good idea," said Patricia.

They all stood up and got ready to leave.

"We can't leave the beach like this!" Prashan said looking around at the mess.

"Neat freak… trust him!" Kaia whispered to Ilene.

She tilted her head down and bit on her bottom lip so she wouldn't start laughing.

"Why don't you make it all disappear?" Miella said, oblivious to Kaia's snide comment.

Prashan did what Miella suggested and his creator turned purple.

As they headed back to the cottage, they divided into two groups. Kaia and Ilene, in front leading the way. Conor, Miella, Patricia and Prashan strolling behind at a leisurely pace.

"Earlier on you asked me a question. I don't mind answering it now, but please don't repeat it to those two in front. I'll tell them when I believe they deserve to know." Patricia said.

"Of course I won't say anything! Kaia's my cousin but I don't tell him everything!" Miella replied.

Conor and Prashan also agreed to keep what Patricia was about to say to themselves.

"I flipped out the other night because I hate bullies. My brother died because of bullies. Our family moved from Paris to London when I was four and my brother was nine. When he started school he used to get teased because he was the new kid and because he had a strong French accent.

I never had any problems probably because I was so young when we moved, but unfortunately for my brother, the older he got the worse the bullying got! I remember mum always having to go to the school to see the teachers, they tried to help but it wasn't enough.

When I was nine and Pierre was fourteen, he had just finished PE and a group of boys started picking on him. He tried to run away from them but slipped, banged his head and fell unconscious. He never woke up. My parents both became really depressed and blamed themselves for not having done more.

It was hard for me too. I felt I no longer existed to them because they were so upset about losing my brother. I started doing stupid things like getting into fights, stealing, smoking and drinking in order to get some attention but it never worked and I made things worse for them.

Mum eventually had a breakdown and dad had to look after her. There was a really kind nurse in the hospital looking after mum, Zophia of course, and also around the same time I became good friends with a new girl in my class, Tania. When they told me who they were and what they wanted me to become I jumped at the chance. I know my parents love me but they had forgotten about me.

I think Zophia may have told me the same secret she told you Prashan because I can deal with his death better now, knowing what I do. I guess we'll never find out as we have promised to never discuss it!" Patricia teased.

"I'm sorry I get so angry with Kaia but do you now understand why I do?" asked Patricia.

Miella nodded, she was deep in thought. It was only after hearing these stories she realised how lucky she had been. She felt guilty for all the times she used to moan and kick up a fuss, thinking her life was unfair because she was asked to do something normal like tidying up her bedroom.

Patricia interrupted her thoughts.

"Prashan I know you said you dislike people arguing and Miella I know it must be hard for you to just sit there and not defend Kaia, so I promise to try to control my temper from now on."

"Thanks," replied Prashan.

Miella noticed they were taking a long time returning to the hut, but she didn't mind as it was nice being outdoors and the trees were providing a much needed shade from the sun, along with a nice gentle breeze.

She wanted to ask Conor about himself but wasn't sure if she was ready for yet another intense story but as she knew she'd find out eventually, she decided to take the risk, "So Conor, how do you feel about telling us a little bit about yourself?"

"There's nothing much to say really. I'm the youngest of five children and we come from a small town in Ireland. My family are great. All my brothers and sisters who are much older than me have stayed in the town and are married, some with children of their own. I'm nearly fifteen and I just knew I wanted to do something different with my life, like travel and see what the world has to offer.

Our school had organised an exchange trip with a school in London and I jumped at the chance to go. I ended up staying with a lady called Zophia and her adopted grandson Christopher.

You all know what happens next so I won't go into it but I ended up here on the island with Christopher for a while and then met all of you. In the short time that I've met all of you, I think I've had more excitement and seen more action than I would have in six months back home," he joked.

Miella was relieved to hear what Conor had to say. It was comforting knowing that she and Kaia were not the only ones to have led happy lives.

"Is it me or have we been walking for a long time?" Patricia asked.

"The thought had crossed my mind earlier on," Miella admitted.

"KAIA! ILENE! WAIT FOR US!" Miella yelled.

They stopped and the others jogged to catch up to them.

"I think we might be lost," said Miella.

"We realised that a little while ago but thought we would find our way back before any of you noticed." Kaia replied.

"Wait a minute! This is the same one! I'm sure of it!" Miella stated.

"The same what?" Kaia asked.

"This plant! This blue plant, look at it! When I left this morning I noticed it because it was so different. Its leaves are blue, have you ever seen that before?"

"That's great, fantastic news! You noticed a plant that's different. Really, I'm very happy for you," he said sarcastically. "Now tell me, *how* that is going to help us?"

"Shut up Kaia! If you let me finish what I was saying without trying to be too smart, you would have heard me say that the hut was right behind the plant. I stood next to this plant this morning!"

"Miella, a building just can't disappear into thin air!" Kaia replied.

"Don't forget where we are! I'm sure anything could happen on this island!" Conor replied.

As soon as he said that a silver envelope suddenly appeared on the plant. Ilene grabbed the envelope and ripped it open, "It's blank! There's nothing on it!"

"Not any more… look!" Prashan said.

Ilene held the piece of paper out in front of her for everyone to see and words started to appear on it. It was like someone was typing them out on a keyboard and the screen was the sheet of paper. It read;

Future Riconians!

As you can see, the hut has disappeared!
You all know now how to use the creator to provide you with the basics (and a few luxuries, the chocolate cake - Kaia) but now things are going to get much more challenging.
You will need to work as a team and help one another to get through the tests ahead of you! There have also been a few concerning incidents. If these continue, life will become more unpleasant for all of you, so you need to stop!
Your instructions are to listen out for the creek, follow it north and when you reach the end, the next stage of your journey will begin.

Good Luck!

Tilly, Appie, Christopher and Tania.

"How exciting is this? Miella you should keep hold of the note as you have a bag. This is excellent... let's go!" Conor said, hyped up.

"I don't know what you are so excited about! Where are we going to sleep tonight?" Ilene asked.

"I'm sure we'll manage to think of something," replied Prashan.

"Look who's talking! Haven't you noticed your toothbrush has disappeared? Oh no! How *are* you going to manage?" Kaia said, trying to impress Ilene.

Ilene sniggered.

"Kaia that was out of order!" Miella said in disgust. She noticed that whenever Kaia said something he thought was rude, smart or funny, he would look to or wait for a reaction from Ilene. Miella's dislike towards Ilene was intensifying.

Conor and Patricia shook their heads in disbelief. Patricia was about to say something, but stopped from doing so, as she remembered her earlier promise.

"I don't know whether your miniscule brain may have noticed, but my creator has now turned purple, meaning that getting my hands on a toothbrush will be one of the easier things it can do!

Kaia... I don't know what your problem is with me and quite honestly I don't care but you had better sort it out. You don't know me well enough to be messing with me. Trust me," replied Prashan menacingly.

"What? Am I supposed to be scared of you now?"

"Kaia... I'm going to do you a massive favour and let it drop, but don't push me! Everyone has their limits and it won't be a pretty picture when I reach mine!" Prashan said, in such a confident and threatening tone of voice that Miella decided to step in immediately.

She knew what Prashan was capable of doing and although she felt Kaia probably deserved a taster, there was no way she was going to let it happen. "Ok, ok that's enough! We need to work together, not against each other! So has anyone seen a creek or heard something sounding like a creek?" Miella asked, trying to ease the tension.

They all shook their heads at the same time.

"I'm going to try something," said Conor. He took his creator out and changed it into a compass. "We have to head that way," he said, pointing in the direction of where the hut once stood.

"Well done! Let's get moving then, or does anyone have any objections?" Miella asked, directing her focus straight at Ilene and Kaia.

Ilene pretended she hadn't noticed Miella's glare but Kaia looked down at the ground with a sheepish expression, not wanting to make eye contact with her.

"Good, we should get moving," she stated.

Conor then turned the compass back into his creator and as soon as he did it changed from blue to purple and then orange.

The six of them walked towards the spot where the hut would have been and carried on further into a part of the island which was new territory to them. They walked in silence, listening out for the sound of the creek and taking great notice of their surroundings to prevent them from getting lost.

"There it is, over there, I can see it," Patricia shouted out excitedly.

Conor, Patricia, Miella, Prashan and Kaia started running excitedly towards the creek. Kaia looked around to see where Ilene was. She was still walking behind. He stopped running and waited for her.

"Come on! Let's try and beat the others," he said.

"Oh please Kaia! What are you getting so excited about? What do you think you're going to find up there…a circus and a marching band? It's just going to be a ditch with water, GREAT! That's something to really get excited and worked up about, isn't it? But please, go ahead Kaia, join the nerd and his buddies. Don't let me stop you!"

"No, I guess you are right. I never really thought about it like that," Kaia replied. When they got to the creek, they saw Miella, Prashan, Conor and Patricia waist deep in water, splashing about and having lots of fun.

"You two, jump in! The water is beautiful, it's so fresh and clean, you can even drink it!" Conor shouted just as Prashan came from behind him and playfully jumped on him.

Kaia started to laugh.

"Kaia the water is really nice and cooling. It's exactly what is needed after our walk in the heat, jump in!" Miella shouted.

Kaia undid the laces on his shoes and started to take his trainers off.

"What are you doing? You can't seriously want to join them!" Ilene said to Kaia as he started to take his socks off.

"But look at how much fun they are all having!"

"Well if you consider jumping about in water as though you are five years old fun then please go ahead and join them," said Ilene disapprovingly.

"I suppose you have a point," he said sounding very disappointed. "What do you feel like doing instead?" Kaia asked, putting his socks and shoes back on.

"I'm quite happy to sit here and watch them make idiots out of themselves."

Miella looked over at them and noticed her cousin sitting miserably next to Ilene.

"Aren't you two going to join us?"

"Nah, we're both a bit tired so we'll just relax over here for a while," Kaia lied.

"Fair enough, but you don't know what you are missing out on!" Miella replied.

She knew Ilene had something to do with him not joining in but thought if he was silly enough to listen to her, then she would leave him too it. She was having far too much of a good time with Patricia, Prashan and Conor.

"We've been in here for quite a while now, we should think about drying off and continue going north," Conor suggested.

"That sounds like a very sensible idea but just before we all get out I think we have time for one more splash," and just as Prashan said that he raised both his hands in the air and slammed them down in the water in Conor's direction.

Conor was drenched!

Patricia and Miella joined in. Conor valiantly tried to defend himself but it was no use! The four of them were laughing so hard that even Kaia, sitting grumpily on the bank, couldn't help but raise a smile.

"Alright, alright, I give up! You guys win! Three against one, what did I do to deserve that?" Conor asked jokingly as he climbed out of the water and on to the bank.

"Ah you did nothing to deserve that, it was just a bit of fun," replied Miella in an awful Irish accent.

"Are you trying to make fun out of the way I speak?" Conor asked, running towards her.

"Nooooo, I'm just messing about with you," she screamed as she tried to run away from him. He caught up with her and the two of them ended up wrestling playfully on the grassing bank.

"They look so pathetic! Look at them rolling around like a couple of pigs in mud!" Ilene said to Kaia, unaware Patricia could hear her.

"You have such a bad attitude problem! Why does it bother you so much to see people having fun?" Patricia asked, trying her hardest to remain calm.

"Oh just shut up and stop eavesdropping on conversations!" Ilene replied.

"You stupid miserable..." but before she could finish Prashan stepped in, "Let it go Patricia, it's just not worth it!"

"You're right! She's not worth the hassle!" Patricia said, as she walked towards Conor and Miella, who were both still trying to get their breaths back after laughing so hard.

"That was bit harsh, what you just said. Don't forget she is my cousin." Kaia said to Ilene as soon as Patricia and Prashan were out of earshot.

"Look Kaia, I never asked you to hang around with me. If you don't like the things I say or do then go and hang about with those weirdoes... I've never needed anyone in my life before and I don't need you or anyone else now!" she said bluntly.

"I never said that, all I was saying… Oh, it doesn't matter. I'd much rather hang around with you than them. We're alike in so many ways and I like being around you." Kaia replied.

"Aww that's so nice of you to say," said Ilene smiling falsely at Kaia.

"Argh! That girl really knows how to wind me up!" Patricia said.

"Why, what happened?" Miella asked.

"Oh nothing, just Ilene being Ilene I suppose," answered Patricia

"Let's just leave it at that!" Prashan added, fearing Patricia would get angry again and start a fight.

"Yeah, just forget it, it's not worth it! I'm soaking, we need to get out of these wet clothes and dry off," Patricia said.

"Why bother when we have these?" Miella said pulling out her creator and changing into a new and dry outfit. The others did the same. Miella looked up at the sky, the sun looked like it was beginning to set so she called Kaia and Ilene over to join them.

"I think we'd better continue before it gets too dark," she said, once they were all gathered together.

All in agreement, they carried on walking up along the bank by the creek.

"I wonder where we're going to sleep tonight…" Patricia said aloud.

"Don't really know. The thought had crossed my mind, especially as it is getting dark and I'm getting tired!" Prashan replied.

"Maybe they'll give us somewhere a bit more luxurious than the hut. I could do with a really nice soak in a Jacuzzi," Ilene said.

"A bath tub would do me just fine!" Patricia said.

"Well I wouldn't expect someone like you to know about the finer things in life!" Ilene replied snobbishly.

"Right, that's it! I have had enough of you!" Patricia said turning around to face Ilene.

"What? Whatcha gonna do?" Ilene challenged Patricia, and then gave her a fierce push.

Without having the time to think about what she was doing, Patricia clenched her right hand into a fist and threw a right hook at Ilene's face. It caught her hard on the cheek and sent her flying.

Kaia and Conor immediately ran over to check on Ilene, who was sitting on the floor looking extremely dishevelled, whilst Miella and Prashan pulled a shocked but still raging Patricia away.

"Maybe that'll teach you to shut up once and for all!" Patricia said, as she shook Prashan and Miella off her, and walked away taking deep breaths trying to calm down.

"Are you ok?" Miella asked Ilene, who was now standing up and dusting herself off.

"FINE… Just keep her well away from me!" Ilene said also raging.

As soon as those words were spoken, the clear skies turned cloudy and there was a heavy downpour of rain followed by thunder and a flash of lightening.

"No way is this happening now!" Kaia yelled above the noise.

"Do you remember what the mentors wrote in the note about life being unpleasant for all of us if the arguing continued? I think this is exactly what they meant," Conor said sounding fed-up.

"Well what are we going to do?" Miella asked.

"We need some umbrellas otherwise we're all going to get drenched," Ilene replied.

"Are you crazy?" Conor shouted, as the roar of thunder got closer and louder.

"There's lightning, we're surrounded by trees and you want to put an umbrella in the air, do you know how dangerous that is?"

"Well do you have any better ideas?" Ilene asked

"We need to find or make some kind of shelter!"

By now, not only was the rain heavier, and the thunder louder, but there was also a strong wind blowing fiercely to contend with.

"We need to stick together and use our creators to make some kind of shelter. Come on... we need to catch up with Patricia and Prashan..." Conor said.

"I'm not going anywhere near that girl!" Ilene replied.

"This isn't the time to be stubborn. It's not just about you! We all need shelter and we all need to work together to get it. Now come on!" Miella ordered. The four of them ran to catch up with Patricia and Prashan.

"PATRICIA, PRASHAN WAIT..." Conor yelled. Prashan and Patricia stopped and waited.

"We need shelter and the only way we'll get it is by using our creators together!" Conor shouted but was still bearly audible due to the noise from the extreme weather

Patricia looked at Ilene hesitantly.

"Patricia, Ilene please put your differences aside for now." Miella pleaded.

A flash of lightning struck a tree about fifty metres away from them. They all jumped with fright and watched the tree go up in flames.

"Come on! Please! Think of a cave or something to provide us with shelter!" Conor said in desperation.

They all stood in a circle holding their creators in one hand and placed them together in the centre. As they did, the rain clouds quickly dispersed and the sky returned to the way it was before, clear and with the sun setting. The tree which was on fire now stood tall as if nothing had happened.

"THANK YOU!" Kaia shouted tilting his head up towards the sky.

"You do realise that just happened because of you two fighting? It's not fair for us to get dragged into your mess. Ilene, all you do is moan about everything, sit around and sulk. While I'm on the subject... I don't know what you are saying to my cousin, but leave him alone! Especially if you are going to carry on being an idiot because I don't like the way he acts around you... sort yourself out because we're all in this together and we need to get on with each other to pass!" Miella yelled furiously.

"Miella, I can speak for myself and stop picking on her. Your friend Patricia also had a part to play with what has just happened or have you forgotten that?" Kaia responded.

"Are you blind Kaia? What is wrong with you? What's so appealing about being friends with someone like her?" Miella asked.

"What's wrong with me?" Ilene asked defensively, but with a very aggressive tone of voice.

"Where do I start? Look, I really don't want to get into this but all I know is I'm finding it really difficult to see anything right with you at the moment!" Miella replied.

"STOP!" yelled Prashan.

"EVERYONE just stop the arguing. *Please!* It's getting out of hand. Let's just change into some dry clothes, walk on for a bit, find somewhere to sleep for the night and discuss this in the morning when everyone is calmer."

The others agreed and carried on walking along the creek for at least one hour in complete silence. By now the sky had become almost pitch black with the exception of the stars and the moon providing some light.

"Is it me or can anyone else see that light ahead of us?" Conor asked.

"No… you're right! Something's there, it looks like a fire," replied Patricia.

They all walked quickly towards the light. When they got closer, they saw a large tent and an open fire with two very large logs on either side.

"I guess this is where we will be spending the night! So much for the five star accommodation I was imagining," Conor joked.

Miella looked inside the tent, "At least we have sleeping bags!"

"Night guys, I'm exhausted so I'm going to go straight to bed."

"See you in the morning, Patricia." Miella answered, smiling understandingly.

Everyone else gathered around the fire eating food they had used the creator to make. No one was making much conversation.

As soon as Prashan and Conor finished eating, they decided to go for a walk. Ilene did the same but headed off in a different direction, on her own.

"Kaia I'm glad the two of us are alone. I've been meaning to say something to you all afternoon... I don't like the way you act and behave around Ilene."

"Oh Miella! You said this earlier and I don't know why you're so jealous of my friendship with Ilene. Just get over it!" Kaia said angrily and walked off in the same direction as Ilene. He saw her outline ahead, "Ilene, wait!"

"Kaia, what do you want?"

"It's Miella! She has a real problem with us two being friends, I think she's jealous and I'm just fed up of it!"

"Oh, is that it?" Ilene replied.

"What do you mean by that? Doesn't it bother you that she doesn't like you? I mean you heard all the stuff she said earlier!"

"Kaia, let's get one thing straight! The two of us are not friends. How can we be? I've only known you for a couple of days and quite frankly... she has a point! You have been following me around like a bad smell all day long and you're still here, even after I told you I wanted to be left alone," she said, looking straight at his eyes, in a very cold and unemotional tone of voice.

"Is that really how you feel?"

"I wouldn't have said it if I didn't mean it! Go away!"

Kaia didn't know what to feel! He was shocked and upset but mainly angry! Really angry at himself for acting the way he had, and for treating Miella badly. He walked back to the camp and headed straight for the tent.

By now Patricia, Miella, Prashan and Conor were asleep in their sleeping bags. Kaia climbed into his and closed his eyes.

V

"OUCH, I just leant on a stone! Where's the tent? Where have all the sleeping bags gone?" Miella shouted in surprise, and waking everyone up by doing so.

Miella looked around. The sun shone brightly down on them. She noticed Ilene was lying on the floor close to where the fire had been the night before, but now there was nothing in its place except grass. In fact they were all lying on the grass and Miella had the extra discomfort of a stone. Everything had disappeared, even the two logs they were sitting on the night before.

"What happened?" Conor asked looking around in disbelief.

"I don't know! I'm guessing it's the mentors' idea of a wake up call!" Prashan said.

"Oh well, at least it is not raining," said Conor trying to sound upbeat.

Patricia stood up and walked over to Ilene, "Morning," she said nervously.

"Morning," Ilene replied, surprised that Patricia had approached her.

"Didn't you sleep in the tent last night?"

"No, I went for a long walk and did quite a lot of thinking. Everyone was asleep when I got back so I thought it would be best if I slept here by the fire. It was warm enough."

"Listen, I have been doing a lot of thinking too. Can we start over again? We are constantly at each other and it's pointless because we don't know each other at all. Plus, we are making life very uncomfortable for everyone around us," said Patricia.

"It's funny you say that because I was thinking the same. I know I've been a nightmare... it's just that this is all new to me. I'm not used to being around people and making friends because I've always moved around... I'm sorry!"

"Me too," replied Patricia.

Ilene put her hand out, "Truce?"

Patricia shook it and replied "Truce!"

Ilene then stood up and walked over to the others who were still seated on the floor.

"I'd really like to apologise to everyone here. I'm sorry for the way I have been behaving. There will not be anymore repeats of what happened yesterday, I promise! Kaia, I'm sorry about what I said last night. I really didn't mean any of it. Are we still friends?"

"Yeah, we're still friends," replied Kaia, smiling.

"Miella, I guess it's my turn now. I'm sorry for the way I spoke to you before," Kaia said.

"Already forgotten about!" Miella replied.

"All of this is too far too much for me!" Conor said jokingly, as though he was about to cry, "Pass the tissues, Prashan."

Prashan held up an imaginary box of tissues.

"There you go," he said pretending to sound just as upset as Conor.

They both then pretended to dab imaginary tears with the imaginary tissues and sniffed.

"Very funny guys!" Ilene said laughing at the two of them.

"I guess we have found the comedians of the group," added Patricia also laughing.

"Oh well! At least they are putting a smile on all our faces which can't be a bad thing, even if their jokes are!" Miella said, laughing too.

"Time to head off again, I'd say, what does everyone else think?" Miella asked.

"You're right. I can't wait to see what exactly it is they have planned for us at the end of our little adventure," said Conor.

"Well there is only one way to know and the sooner we get going the sooner we find out!" Prashan replied.

The six of them got ready quickly and continued on their journey.

The scenery was incredible! They were still walking along the creek which ran parallel to the crystal clear blue ocean and blended in perfectly with the bright blue cloudless sky. The sun shone brightly and illuminated the tropical trees and plants on the mountainous part of the island which they were now heading towards.

They walked, mainly in silence, lost in their thoughts, enjoying the sound of the birds singing around them and absorbing all the novelties the environment had to offer. Time had passed by really quickly and they had no idea they had been walking non-stop for over four hours.

"What was that noise?"

"What noise, Kaia? I can't hear anything apart from the birds," Miella replied.

"SHHH, listen carefully," he said, sounding concerned.

They all stopped to listen.

"There it is again, can you hear it?" Kaia asked.

"I heard something! I don't know what it was though, it's coming from over there," said Prashan, pointing towards a part of the island about a hundred meters away.

It was more of a woodland area than where they currently were. The trees looked tall and menacing and the noise, they could all now hear, was not a very welcoming one.

"What should we do?" Ilene asked.

"We were told to walk along by the creek and maybe that's what we should do. Just carry on... what do you think?" Miella asked.

"That noise sounds like some kind of monster roaring. I don't think we should go over there," said Patricia.

"The fact that I don't know what is making that noise scares me. We should just get as far away from here and as quickly as we can!" Conor added.

They started to walk fast, unsure whether they had done the right thing. They heard the noise again, and it frightened them as they had never heard anything like that before. The area it was coming from was also terrifying; it was extremely dark because of the tall trees blocking the sunlight. The faster they tried to walk away from it, the louder and more intense the noise seemed to get.

"I can't do this! I have to go back and see what was making that noise. It might be in trouble and need help," said Prashan.

"I'm not too sure if that would be such a good idea!" Ilene added.

"Ok, I'm going back! You don't need to come with me, I'll catch up with the rest of you later."

"I'm coming with you Prashan," said Patricia

"We will all come with you!" asserted Miella

"Huh?" Kaia said in surprise.

"I mean… I'm not scared or anything… I just think it would be a bad idea,"

"Kaia, we are all just as afraid as you but we simply cannot ignore the fact that someone or something might be in trouble and need our help," said Prashan.

"Who said I was scared? I'm not! Come on then… let's go!" Kaia said, pushing himself to the front and taking charge.

"Ok Kaia, you lead the way, seeing as though *you* are the only one amongst us who isn't afraid of what we are going to find," said Miella, knowing he was just as frightened as everyone else.

They turned around and walked towards the direction the noise was coming from. Kaia maintained the lead and the others followed directly behind him. The closer they got, the darker it got and the louder the noise became. It was a petrifying sound which echoed through the trees. It sounded like a loud groan combined with an extremely loud roar followed by a very loud high pitched squeal. Kaia felt as though his heart was about to beat out of his chest, but did not want to admit his fear. He slowed down.

"It's coming from further in there… I can't see very well, there isn't much light," he said, partly as an excuse to slow down in the hope that someone might decide to turn back.

"Hold on, why don't we turn our creators into torches?" Prashan asked.

'Argh! Trust him to say that!' thought Kaia, but he didn't dare say it out loud because everyone had supposedly decided to be friends. Kaia really had no idea why Prashan bothered him so much, he just did! His thoughts were interrupted by the noise which was getting louder and louder.

"It's coming from over there… just behind that large tree!" Kaia said with his voice trembling, he had now slowed down so much that Patricia was in front.

"We need a plan as we don't know what's behind the tree. It could be really dangerous." Patricia whispered.

"I have an idea," whispered Ilene.

"First, we switch the torches off so whatever it is can't see us. There's just about enough light to get us around those trees on the right to get a closer and better look yet still be able to run to safety, should we need to. We need to know what it before we can do anything to help. Is everyone ok with that?"

They all nodded back at her.

"Good! Now follow me but please try to make as little noise as you can!" Ilene said, taking charge to ensure they all walked very slowly and not draw attention to themselves. With each footstep the children made, they had to be certain not to step on any twigs as the sound would echo. The children noticed that the screeching and roaring wasn't happening as often as before and hoped it was because whatever was making the noise was tiring.

'CRACK!'

Someone stepped on a twig and their weight caused it to noisly break in half! The roaring started up again, louder than before.

"It knows we are here," whispered Kaia.

"Shhhhh! We're nearly there and even if it does, I'm pretty sure we are behind it, so we can still run if we have to," Patricia whispered back, as they all manoeuvred around the last tree.

"OK… I think we are at a safe enough distance to put our torches back on and see what it is. Ok… after three, one… two… three…" Miella gasped in horror.

"What is it?"

"It looks like a panther! But panthers are black all over aren't they? This one has a white patch just under its neck and chest. I don't think panthers usually have that. Well whatever it is, it needs our help," Patricia replied.

"What? Are you mad? Great idea Patricia, we help it and it repays us by eating us! There is no way I am going anywhere near that... that thing!"

"Look at it properly Kaia! It's in agony!"

Miella shone her torch on the animal for Kaia to have a good look, she noticed his eyes were firmly shut when they first shone their torches.

"Well big deal! It's trapped in some vines but I'm sure it will free itself somehow," Kaia said, very frustrated by being the only one wanting to carry on with the task.

"Look carefully," said Ilene, shining the light on its hind legs. The right one which was closest to them was badly broken with the bone sticking out and blood pouring out from it.

"Oh!" Kaia exclaimed, finally realising why the animal was in pain.

"Well what can we do? None of us are vets," he said, trying his hardest to be sympathetic.

"Remember what Appie said about having the ability to heal other Riconians, maybe we should try with the animal," suggested Conor.

"How can we get close enough without it attacking us?" Prashan asked.

"We may not need to get close to it. We might be able to help it from where we are. Let's try... hopefully, it should work," said Conor.

"Ok then, let's give it a go!" Kaia replied reluctantly.

The six of them stood in a circle facing each other and held on to their creators with both their hands. They all closed their eyes and concentrated for about a minute.

The animal roared loudly. Miella opened her eyes.

"Nothing has happened," she said disappointedly.

The others opened their eyes too.

"Ok let's try again. Focus hard. It has to work this time," said Conor.

They all tried again. This time it was Patricia who was the first to open her eyes.

"Still no change I'm afraid," she said sounding just as disappointed as Miella had earlier.

"There's no point in us carrying on with this. We should just accept the fact that there is nothing else we can do for it apart from trying to put it out of its misery," Kaia said trying to be practical.

"What do you mean? Kill it?" Prashan asked in disbelief.

"Well if that is what we have to do, then so be it!"

"Kaia forget any ideas you have about killing the animal! There *has* to be a way of doing this. There is no way I am going to quit easily. We need to think of another way... everyone think please!" Prashan pleaded.

"Ok, this sounds crazy but I think it is the only way to help. The animal looks very weak tangled up in those vines. Judging from the amount of blood lost and with its leg in such a bad state it cannot run after us... I guess what I'm trying to say, without scaring you, is we need to touch it for us to be able to heal it. Like how we fixed the tap in the cottage," said Prashan.

"You know what... you managed to fix the tap fine without me and I'm sure you'll do just as well this time. There is no way I'm going near that thing! We don't even know what it is, forget it!"

"Kaia! Listen to yourself! We're all scared but it has to be done, and it's not like the tap when we could have called for your help later. This animal could attack us and we can't afford to take any chances. We do this together, if we do it. The animal is completely tangled up in those vines... there is no possible way for it to be able to run after us. Kaia we need you to do this with us. Are you in or not?" Miella asked sternly.

Everyone looked at Kaia

"We are all scared!" Ilene said. The others nodded their heads in agreement.

"Ok... count me in..." Kaia said nervously.

"Thank you," said Miella

"This is the plan; we walk slowly behind it and gently place one of our hands near its injured leg... make sure your creators are already in your free hand and then concentrate and focus like we did just now. As soon as its leg is better run back the same way we came in. Don't turn around, just run!" Prashan said. "Any questions?" he added, trying to sound as calm as he could with his heart racing through a combination of adrenaline and fear.

No one answered.

"Let's do it then!"

They all set off slowly behind Prashan. The closer they got to the animal, the more obvious it was that they were dealing with a panther. Prashan was the first to put his hand on its leg near the wound. The others placed their hands down less than a second after Prashan and did as he had instructed.

"It's working! We're doing it!" Miella exclaimed, almost crying with relief and happiness.

The bone started moving back into place and the torn flesh just appeared to heal itself. The panther let out a massive roar.

"We've done it! Now run!" Prashan yelled.

They ran back as fast as they could. All except Prashan, he remained behind on purpose. There was no way he could leave the panther tangled up the way it was. The panther had collapsed from exhaustion. Prashan decided it would be a perfect opportunity to free it. He turned his creator into a massive pair of shears and chopped away at the vines. There was nothing to stop the panther from attacking Prashan.

VI

Patricia was the first to run back into the part of the island that the creek was running through. She turned around to see who was behind her, it was Conor.

"I can't believe we just did that!" Patricia said, exhausted from running.

"That was mad! Completely crazy but amazing, I feel like I'm on top of the world!" Conor said, with adrenaline still pumping through his body.

85

Ilene, Miella and Kaia all came running out at pretty much the same time.

"I can't believe we managed to pull that off!" Miella said, wiping the sweat off her forehead whilst trying to catch her breath.

"Hold on, where's Prashan?" Kaia asked, slightly worried as he was nowhere to be seen.

"I'm sure he'll be out any second now," replied Miella, impressed that Kaia was bothered enough to care.

They all stood facing the woods. There was still no sign of Prashan and they started to fret.

"He should be out by now..." said Miella.

"I'm going back in to get him!" Patricia exclaimed, ready to turn around and run back.

"Wait just a minute longer and we'll all go with you!"

"No need Kaia... there he is!" Conor said sounding extremely relieved.

"Keep running towards the Creek, don't stop now!" Prashan shouted as he ran towards them.

"Why did it take you so long to come out of there? We were really worried about you," said Patricia.

"Just keep running... I'll explain later!"

When they finally reached the creek they stopped running and tried to catch their breath.

"What happened back there?" Patricia asked, slightly concerned.

"I know you'll all think I'm crazy but I couldn't leave the panther tied up. I had to free it!" Prashan answered, still out of breath.

"What if it comes after us now that it is free?" Kaia asked.

"I doubt it will but just to be on the safe side, we shouldn't wait around. We should get as far away from here and as quickly as possible!" Prashan replied.

All in agreement, they carried on with their task, walking briskly with adrenaline still rushing through their bodies.

"Oh no! Where is it? I can't find it!" Prashan said, furiously patting himself down.

"What can't you find?" Conor asked

"My creator! I think I may have dropped it when I ran away from the panther earlier on."

"Well forget going back for it. There's no way I'm doing that," Kaia said.

"No one asked you to!" Prashan replied sharply.

"Good because I won't!" Kaia said back in just as sharp a tone of voice.

"Time-out! We're all doing so well getting on with each other, can we keep that going please?" Ilene asked in a jovial tone of voice.

"Yeah… if we can do it then so can you! Prashan you can stop looking for your creator. It fell out of your pocket when you were running earlier on. I was waiting to see how long it would take before you realised it had gone," said Patricia, laughing at the frenzy Prashan had worked himself into.

"That's not funny! I really thought I was going to have to go back. Patricia you should have told me this earlier, instead of letting me panic like that!" Prashan said, unable to see the funny side.

"Well let it be a good lesson for you to learn, and this way you won't lose it again," she said handing it back to him.

"Wow, its pink now!" Prashan happily observed.

"When I saw that yours was pink I checked mine, it's the same," said Patricia.

The others then checked to see what colour theirs had changed to.

"We're all the same now," said Patricia.

"Finally, Kaia and I have caught up with all of you! I wonder how powerful these things are now.

Miella, I hope you don't mind me asking, but what else do you have in that bag of yours? Ever since we met, I've noticed you keep your bag close to you and rarely out of sight," Ilene said after putting her creator back in its pouch and then in her pocket.

"No, I don't mind telling you," replied Miella, and told them the story behind the photo.

"Zophia told me to always keep hold of this," said Patricia, pointing to a gold bracelet on her wrist.

"It was the last birthday present I got from my family before my brother died," she said, touching it gently with her right hand.

"You have a brother that died? I'm sorry to hear that. Zophia told me to hold on to this," said Ilene, pointing to a locket around her neck. She opened it up, one half contained a tiny picture of her and on the other side was a photo of another woman.

"They are photos of me and my mother," she said as she closed the locket.

"Do you know what I've just realised... I don't know much about most of you. That has to change and it starts with you," said Ilene, linking arms with Patricia. The two of them then walked off slightly ahead of everyone else.

"I think we all have a reminder of our lives before we met the Riconians. My watch was also a birthday present from my family," said Conor

"Not all of us, but then again, there is nothing I have to go back for," said Prashan, not even slightly bothered by this.

They continued walking for a little while longer. As daylight dwindled, they realised they must have been walking for quite some time.

"We should find somewhere to settle down for the night. I don't feel like walking much more," said Miella.

"Me too, I think we should use our creators to make a place for us to spend the night in," said Kaia.

"This thing must be quite powerful now! Where would you like to sleep? A mansion, a palace or perhaps a castle?" Conor asked half joking and half being serious.

"I guess we could make one of those, couldn't we?"

Kaia was excited by the thought of the amount of power his creators now had.

"I'd quite like for us to re-create the camp we had last night. I think it would be fun to sit around the fire and eat melted marshmallows. *Yum,* just thinking about it makes my mouth water," said Kaia.

"You do realise we could have as much comfort and luxury as we want tonight don't you? Are you sure you would honestly rather sleep in a tent than a nice warm bed?" Conor asked, very surprised by Kaia's choice.

"I think it's a great idea, sounds like fun," replied Miella, laughing at the surprised expression on Conor's face.

"A camp it is... unless anyone has any objections?" Conor asked.

The others seemed happy with the decision.

All of a sudden a fire appeared at a spot not too far from them.

"That should get the ball rolling," laughed Conor as everyone jumped in surprise.

They all joined in and within a matter of minutes they had created an exact replica of the camp they were all in the night before. They sat down on some logs facing the fire.

"I've just realised we haven't eaten since this morning," said Conor

"I just want my marshmallows," said Kaia, licking his lips. "I'll go and try to find some twigs so we can do this properly and you guys sort out dinner. How does that sound?"

"You know you could just use the creator to make some twigs appear here."

"Yes Mimi, I know but where's the fun in that? I'd like to do this the proper way."

"Do you mind if I come along?" asked Prashan.

Kaia's initial reaction was to say yes, but seeing as though everyone else was making a big effort to get along with each other, he thought he should do the same. He also realised he had never actually given Prashan a chance or knew very much about him.

"No, of course not, let's go," said Kaia.

"Maybe we should try by those trees over there," said Prashan pointing at some trees about twenty meters ahead of them.

It was really dark now and as they were a fair distance away from the camp, the fire no longer provided them with much light.

"Did you hear that?"

"Not again! Remember what happened the last time you heard strange noises?" Prashan joked.

Kaia laughed. "Thankfully it's not the same noise this time. It just sounded like someone was following us."

"I didn't hear anything but if anyone is following us it would probably be Conor trying to play a joke or scare us," commented Prashan, trying to put Kaia's mind at ease. "Let's use this, just in case," said Prashan, turning his creator into a torch. He shone it around them checking to see if anyone else was nearby.

"Conor we know it's you, the game's up mate, come out," said Kaia joking about.

"I guess he isn't following us," said Prashan, after Conor had failed to appear.

"Let's just get those twigs and get out of here!"

They walked over to the trees. There were a few twigs just the right length for toasting marshmallows. As Kaia bent down to pick them up he felt something land on his shoulder. "What was that?"

"What? Did you hear the noise again?"

"No... something just landed on my shoulder and it better not be what I think it is," replied Kaia, with his voice trembling.

Prashan shone the torch on Kaia's shoulders.

"Err Kaia, whatever you do, don't move! Stay still!" Prashan saw a large spider he was sure was poisonous on Kaia's left shoulder.

"What is it Prashan?" Kaia asked, with his voice trembling even more than it was before.

"I mean it, stay still! Don't move! It's... It's... It's just a little spider," said Prashan, weary of Kaia's reaction if he told him the truth.

"Get it off me!" Kaia pleaded, with tears now rolling down his face.

"Ok, hold on!" Prashan picked up a couple of pieces of wood. One was a twig and the other was a larger piece of a branch.

"Kaia you have to try and stop shaking! Earlier today you touched a massive panther. This is a tiny spider! Plus every time you move there's more chance of the spider moving or even worse biting!"

"Ok, I'll try."

Prashan placed the larger piece of wood under the spider, gently prodding and pushing it with the twig, he moved it onto the branch.

"Ok, Kaia, it's off you!" Prashan said, walking away from where they were both standing, and gently placing the branch on the ground.

Kaia dropped the twigs he was holding and frantically wiped his shoulder whilst running away. Prashan followed him and as soon as they were far away from the spider, Kaia stopped. "Thank you," he said to Prashan. "Ever since I was a toddler I've been petrified of spiders. I just can't seem to get rid of that fear. I hate them!"

"Well if I'm honest, it wasn't little… it was quite big and I think a poisonous one! But look at it this way, you've dealt with one of the biggest of the bunch and survived!" Prashan said, trying to be helpful, and stop him from feeling embarrassed.

"I never thought about it like that!"

"Listen if you are worried about me telling the others about what just happened here… don't! I promise I won't!"

"Thank you Prashan," Kaia said humbly.

"As for the twigs, well we have the creator, the others will be none the wiser," said Prashan, then suddenly looking around and feeling very uneasy.

"Are you ok?" Kaia asked, slightly disturbed by Prashan's odd behaviour.

"No, not really! I heard something just then and I don't know what it is… let's just get out of here and quickly!"

"What's wrong mate?" Kaia shone the torch on Prashan. He looked terrified. He then waved the torch around, trying to see if anyone was around.

"I heard a very strange noise. It sounded like really loud and heavy breathing. I don't know what it was but I don't think we should stick around to find out what it is either... we need to get back to camp to warn the others."

As they approached the camp they slowed down slightly, the light coming from the fire made things seem less scary.

"It's about time you got back, we've nearly finished all the food. Where are the twigs?" Conor asked.

"Hold on, something's wrong! I've seen that look on Kaia's face plenty of times before... What is it?"

"Not too sure Mimi... Prashan said he heard something and whatever it was has seriously freaked him out!"

"Are you ok?" Miella asked Prashan, as the others gathered around, worried about what he had heard.

"Yeah, I think so! It was just a really strange noise, like heavy breathing or huffing or something," he replied vaguely.

"Uh oh... I think I know exactly what it is!" Patricia said with her voice trembling and her eyes fixed on the bushes just behind Prashan and Kaia. Patricia started to slowly walk backwards, away from whatever it was that caught her attention. The others all followed her gaze and froze with fear when they saw what it was. The panther was back and was walking slowly towards them.

"What do we do?" Conor asked in fear.

"Back away and start splitting up," replied Prashan.

They all walked slowly away from the panther, which in turn was walking slowly towards them; all of a sudden it started running towards Prashan. The others started to scream and shout.

The panther jumped up at Prashan, knocking him straight down to the ground and then started licking him.

"Eugh! He's kissing you!" Patricia exclaimed, in a combination of disgust and relief.

The panther stopped licking Prashan and walked over to Miella.

"Oh no! Tell it to get away from me... I don't want it anywhere near me," she said, backing away with her arms outstretched, ready to protect herself.

"It's not going to attack you Miella. If it was it would have done so by now," said Prashan, wiping the saliva off his face with the bottom of his t-shirt.

"Just stroke it and it should leave you alone," he added.

"What? Are you nuts? I'm not stroking a panther," screeched Miella.

Kaia took a deep breath and walked towards the panther and Miella. He then put his hand out and stroked its back.

"See, if I can do it, then so can you," he said to her.

Miella stopped backing away and stroked the panther.

"So what does all this mean? That we have a panther as a pet?" Ilene asked in disbelief

"I guess so," replied Prashan

"You do know this is your fault Prashan," said Conor.

"I guess," he replied, bemused by the whole situation.

"Well good because you can walk behind him with the pooper scooper!" Conor said laughing.

"Ha ha, very funny," replied Prashan, laughing along with him.

"Seriously though, what are we going to do with him?" Conor asked.

"What can we do? If he stays, then I suppose we feed him so that we don't get eaten, and if he goes, he goes," replied Prashan.

"Err... Hello people! What are we going to do with him? I don't think it would be such a good idea to leave him the way he is with all of us asleep," said Kaia.

"Maybe we should tie him to something... I know I'd sleep a lot better knowing I wasn't going to be breakfast," said Prashan.

"Ok so how are we going to do this?" Kaia asked.

"Leave it to me," replied Prashan.

A thick rope appeared. It was attached to its neck and connected to a large and sturdy wooden post firmly stuck into to the ground.

"Wow, well done! You really are getting the hang of using the creator now aren't you?" Kaia said as he held his in his hand.

93

"What colour is yours now?" he asked curiously.

"It's still pink! You would think that after everything we went through today, they would have at least turned it red out of some kind of compassion!" Prashan joked and yawned at the same time.

The two of them then entered the tent to join the others.

VII

"WAKE UP! Guys, wake up and have a look at this!" Conor shouted, poking his head into the tent.

"This had better be worth waking me up for," said Ilene, whilst rubbing her eyes.

"Trust me, it is!" he said, jumping up and down excitedly. "Come on everyone, WAKE UP!"

They all clambered out of their sleeping bags, too tired to get worked up over whatever was getting Conor so excited, but curious enough to want to have a look.

"I can't see what he is getting so worked up for," said Kaia, half asleep as he poked his head out of the tent.

"Oh look!" Prashan pointed over to the wooden post, "The panther's gone," he said.

"No that's not what I'm talking about. Look behind you," said Conor.

They all turned around to see their tent at the bottom of a path that led to an enormous mansion.

"There is no way that was there last night!" Miella said, unable to believe her eyes.

"Look over there!" Conor said. pointing at the creek.

"We're at the end! Wow, I can't believe it! Was it like that last night?" Miella asked.

"It may well have been. It was really dark when we got here but I had noticed the creek was getting narrower and shallower," replied Patricia.

"Ok, enough talking! Let's go and check this house out!" Conor exclaimed excitedly, and then started to sprint up the path.

The others ran right behind him with big smiles on their faces.

They all paused at the front door, to catch their breaths, and saw a note attached to it;

Well done to all of you for getting this far so quickly! You have nearly finished the first part of your training. Your reward for having done so well is inside the house.

Enjoy yourselves! But remember, there is still much to do.

Tilly, Appie, Christopher and Tania.

"Nearly finished? I wonder what else they have planned for us," Miella thought out aloud.

"Who cares right now? Let's see what's inside," said Kaia about to open the door.

"STOP!" Miella yelled.

"What?" Kaia asked, letting go of the handle

"Kaia we need to prepare ourselves in case this is a trick, and part of our training!"

"She could be right!" Conor said, sounding disappointed.

"Only one way to find out..." said Kaia, and pushed the large door open.

The hallway of the house looked like it was a toy shop. There were toys all over the place.

"NO WAY! This is so cool! Wow... check it out! I was going to ask mum and dad for one of these when we got home," exclaimed Kaia in delight as he picked up a remote-controlled toy car.

"Look at how cool it is! You need to fill it up with petrol, just like a real car. Look at it go!"

Whilst the others ran around the house, checking out the rooms, Miella remained cautious. She had a funny feeling that this was a trap. It all seemed too good to be true, and she was determined to investigate the whole house thoroughly.

She opened the door of the first room she came across. It was a huge games room. There was a pool table in the middle and computer games machines all around the walls. She shut the door, there was nothing sinister there, she told herself.

She opened the door of the room opposite. It looked like a cinema. There were six large seats, a very large screen, a popcorn and drinks machine, and a cupboard at the back of the room. Miella opened the cupboard to find hundreds of DVDs, a DVD player and right at the top attached to the DVD player was a very large projector.

She couldn't find fault there either, she shut the door, walked out and along the corridor towards a large wooden spiral staircase. Turning right, she saw there were still three more rooms for her to check out downstairs.

She opened the single door directly in front of the staircase, the room was bizarre.

"I knew it," she muttered.

The walls, the floor and the ceiling were covered in a bright blue padded, leathery material and lying in the middle were two strange looking headsets. She carefully picked up and tried on one of the headsets. Disappointed by the realisation it was a virtual games room, she put the headset back down. She made a mental note to try this room first if she ever needed to find Kaia for anything.

She then walked out of that room and into the next one. All she found here was a dining table and small door leading to a small kitchen. As they were able to make whatever they wanted to eat with their creators, she understood straight away why the kitchen was so tiny.

There was one more room downstairs left for her to investigate. From the two huge doors closing it off from the rest of the house, she knew it was goung to to be big. She pushed one of the doors open and in front of her was a massive hall, like a school gym hall. There were football posts at either end of the hall and towering above them were basketball posts.

Miella loved sports, especially football. She used to love playing with her dad, uncle and Kaia.

One side of the gym had large glass panels instead of a wall and one of the panels doubled as a sliding door leading to the garden. Miella opened the door.

In front of her was an enormous heated swimming pool with a large spiral slide, and pretend rocks you could climb on and jump off into the water. A mini bridge separated the main pool from another which had jet machines to spin you around, and make you feel as though you were in a whirlpool. There were also jets on the floor of the pool that made water shoot out like mini-fountains. Miella couldn't wait to jump in. The view from the pool was amazing. They were on the edge of a cliff on the island, over-looking the beautiful blue water, beach and palm trees below. The view along with the heat from the sun and the breeze from the sea left Miella feeling as though she was in paradise.

Still weary of it being a trap, she walked back into the house and found herself at the bottom of the staircase.

"Miella come and check this out!" Kaia called out from upstairs.

"Coming!" replied Miella, walking up the stairs.

There were six rooms in front of her and each one had a name tag on the front of the door. Miella saw Prashan pop his head out from behind his door.

"Come and have a look at my bedroom." Prashan said, with a big smile beaming on his face.

"It's just the way I have always dreamt of having a bedroom,"

Miella walked into his room. It was decorated with superheroes from various different comics. The wallpaper even looked like pages of comics stuck together.

"I can't believe we have our own rooms! I've always had to share, even when I lived with mum. Look, I even have my own bathroom. This place is excellent!" he said jumping up and down on his bed.

"I am really happy for you," she said smiling, as she remembered how hard his life had been.

"Prashan, Kaia called me earlier. I'd better go and see what he wants," she said.

"Ok, see you later," Prashan replied, still jumping up and down.

The next room along was Ilene's. Miella could hear singing and music coming from it. She opened the door and saw Ilene standing in front of a mirror with a microphone in her hand, singing.

Her room was very plain, but still really nice. Miella smiled and was about to shut the door when Ilene noticed her.

"Miella come and join me! I have my own karaoke machine and this room is just the way that I would choose to have my room. It's like a dance studio. I love singing and dancing and look at all this space I have to do it in. Don't just stand there, join me!" Ilene insisted.

"Later, I promise! I just have to see Kaia first."

"Ok then, later on," sang Ilene, holding the microphone in front of her.

Miella shut the door and giggled. She walked past Conor and Patricia's rooms. She decided to check those out later on.

Miella knocked on Kaia's door. He didn't answer so she opened it.

Kaia's room was full of toys. In fact it looked very similar to the one he had back home. Kaia didn't even realise Miella was standing behind him as he was on the floor, busy playing with the remote controlled car.

"Kaia, what did you want?" Miella asked.

"Huh," he said, surprised to see Miella standing above him. "Oh hi Mimi, what's up?"

"I don't know Kaia, you tell me, you called me up here," she replied.

"I did? Oh yeah... I can't remember why! I think it was just to show you my toys," he replied.

Miella laughed. She had seen him in this state plenty of times before and knew there was no point talking to him when he was busy with something, especially his toys.

She walked out of the room without saying anything to him, there was no point as he wouldn't be paying her any attention.

Her room was right at the end of the corridor, facing the top of the staircase. She opened the door, knowing what to expect after seeing Kaia's room. They both had everything they wanted back at home, including their bedrooms the way they wanted, so when she opened the door to find this one similarly decorated, it did not surprise her.

Miella saw an envelope on her bed. She walked over to it and opened it up;

Hello Miella,

Well done for thinking this is a trick. It is always good to be on guard! However this time you can relax, as it isn't! Please enjoy yourself!

Tilly, Appie, Christopher and Tania.

VIII

About two months had passed and they had all gron really close, living in the house together.

The doorbell rang. It had never rung before so they all stopped what they were doing and headed to the front door.

"I wonder who that could be!" Patricia said to Ilene, as she met her at the foot of the stairs. Kaia was the first to get to the door.

"Hi Tilly!"

"Hello Kaia… hi all! Hope you are well."

"Please come on in," said Kaia.

"It's good to see this place is relatively tidy," she said looking around as she walked in.

"It's so easy to keep it clean and tidy with the creator," replied Conor.

"I know! How do you think Ricon always looks as good as it does? Anyway, I'm here to tell you it will soon be time for all of you to return to Ricon as your training here is nearly complete. There is one last test before you can head back. Follow me to the gym hall."

Curious as to what the final test could be, they did as they were told.

"I hope all of you have your creators with you... you know you should never be without them," she reminded them.

They followed Tilly into the gym hall to find Appie, Tania and oddly enough, the panther standing next to Tania.

"Hello boy," said Prashan as he ran up to him and started stroking him.

"Oh come on!" laughed Appie. "Surely you've worked it out by now!" Appie said, still laughing.

"No way," said Miella feeling really silly as she realised what Appie was talking about.

"NOOOO!" Kaia exclaimed, and then started laughing.

"Are you trying to tell me I got so scared for no real reason and what was that broken leg about? NO WAY!" Prashan said in disbelief.

"Could someone *please* explain, I'm confused," admitted Ilene.

The panther changed into a little cat, walked up to Ilene, rubbed his head against her ankle, walked back to Tania and then changed into Christopher.

"That's just too freaky and strange for me to even comment on!" Ilene said.

"I can't believe you guys did that to us! That's so mean and nasty," said Patricia.

"So any guesses as to what your final test will be?" Christopher asked.

They all looked at each other and then their mentors with blank expressions on their faces.

"Ok then, let me tell you! Just as Appie was an old man when he first met Kaia and Miella, and Christopher turned into a panther, you all have to show us you can use your creators to morph into different beings," Tania said.

"How do we do that?" Ilene asked.

"In exactly the same way you use your creators to do other things. Have a clear picture in your mind of what you want to be and focus into turning into it," explained Tania.

"Ok, I'll go first," said Ilene, and turned herself into a really cute puppy. Patricia did the same and the two of them started running around the gym hall, jumping up and down and performing little tricks in front of the mentors.

"Very cute," said Tilly, laughing at their little tricks.

"Do we have to change into animals?" Conor asked.

"No, you can change into any living creature, just not objects," replied Tania.

Conor managed to change himself into an old woman and then transformed into a tiny toddler.

"Well done you've passed too! You can change back now please because I'd rather not have to change any dirty nappies!" Tilly added, laughing

"I'd like to go next," said Miella.

Suddenly there were two Appies in the room.

"How good looking are you now?" Appie said laughing, as he was faced with himself.

"That's weird!" Patricia said out aloud.

"Now change back as there can only be one person as good looking as me!" Appie said cheekily.

"Ok Kaia, you're the last one left. Your turn now," said Tania.

"Ok," said Kaia, looking worried.

As he held his creator in his hand, a bead of sweat fell from his forehead. He looked really nervous!

"It's not difficult, just hold on to the creator and think of whatever it is you want to be," said Miella.

"I know! Thanks Mimi! I can do this… come on!" Kaia said, before turning himself into a massive tarantula.

Prashan and Miella clapped proudly as they both knew how difficult that must have been for him.

"I can't believe I just did that," he said, having transformed back.

"Well done everyone! If you have a look at your creators, you'll see that they have all turned red. They are now at their full strength. This means you are ready for phase two of your training, but we have to head back to Ricon for this. I'm afraid that means saying goodbye to this beautiful house. Don't be too upset as your bedrooms in Ricon are exactly the same as the ones here. We couldn't be horrible and take it *all* away from you," laughed Tilly.

The children were understandably disappointed at having to leave the house but were also excited to see what other adventures they had ahead of them.

"Ok now that your creators are at full strength, you can make your own way back to Ricon by means of something we call zeling. Can you remember what the room you first arrived in looked like?" Tania asked.

They all nodded their heads.

"Great, now what you have to do is close your eyes and imagine you are there."

They all did as told, and one by one, disappeared.

… … …

RICON

I

"Congratulations for zeling back so successfully on your first attempt," said Tilly proudly.

"That was weird! My body felt all tingly and as soon as it stopped I found myself here," exclaimed Conor.

"That's normal, you would have all felt same and after the first few times you get used to the sensation.

Right! Now that we are here, let's get straight on with the next part of your training. Follow me to the Grand Hall where all will become much clearer," said Tilly, leading the children out of the room and down another corridor.

The other mentors were nowhere to be seen.

As soon as they reached the large staircase Tilly stopped.

"The Grand Hall is on the top floor. Luckily for me, I have my wings to get me there but unluckily for you, you'll have to use your feet and run to the top!" Tilly exclaimed, smiling at the unenthusiastic expressions on their faces.

"You want us to run *all* the way there?" Kaia asked, hoping this was another warped Riconian joke.

"I most certainly do! What are you are waiting for? GO!" Tilly ordered. She opened up her wings and flew up the steps ahead of them. As soon as she had reached the top she turned around to see how far away they were, and was surprised at how fast they had caught up with her. Prashan was the first to reach the top, closely followed by the rest.

Tilly looked at all of them and noticed they were in remarkably good shape, not one of them was out of breath!

"Ok, own up now! Who was the first to use their creator to zel up here?" Tilly asked, unsure at first of that really being the case, but knowing it was by their guilty expressions.

"Come on! Whoever it was should just say so now because I'll find out eventually!" Tilly said, trying to sound as stern as possible.

"It was me!"

"Miella! I am surprised!" Tilly exclaimed.

"I guess I thought I was being…"

"Lazy!" Tilly said, finishing off Miella's sentence before she had a chance to do so herself.

"I suppose the rest of you thought it would be a bright idea to copy her?"

They all nodded sheepishly in agreement.

"Honestly! What am I going to do with all of you?" said Tilly, unable to contain her laughter.

"You're not mad?" asked Miella.

"I'm not impressed with you for disregarding my orders but I do think it was quite a clever thing to do and funny you thinking you coud out-smart me... and, if I'm to be honest, you nearly did!" Tilly admitted.

"I promise I won't do anything like that again," said Miella, slightly embarrassed.

"Please don't! There was a reason I wanted you all to run up the steps. I wanted to see what your fitness levels were like as this second part of training is very physical. I have a good mind to send you all running down and back up again but as we don't have the time, I won't!"

Tilly turned to face the large double doors at the entrance to the Grand Hall. As soon as the doors opened, Tilly heard a slight gasp from one of the children.

"Wow, this place is impressive!" Prashan exclaimed.

Tilly smiled. She was fond of all the children but found something about Prashan just slightly more endearing.

As soon as they were all inside, the children's attention was immediately drawn towards the closing doors and the loud click as they locked shut. This was followed by a wide and long rectangular piece of gold coloured metal, the same colour as the floor, lowering itself from a hole in the ceiling down to the ground, acting as a shield to protect the doors.

"Just to let you know, we are not showing off with expensive gold doors. It's a material similar in colour and texture to gold but much stronger than any metal you have ever seen on Earth. It's called orian and nothing can get through it. The extra security is needed on this floor as Zophia's office is through the doors on the other side of the room," explained Tilly as she walked over to a machine situated to the left of the doors. She pressed a few keys on the machine and with a flick of her wrist indicated for the children to gather closer to her.

"You all need to place your hands on the scanner so it can record your prints and allow you entry into rooms which have extra security such as this one.

You'll find orian covering the ceilings, floors, doors and walls of all of these rooms. You'll notice extra security is used only in places which hold a large number of Riconians.

Your bedrooms and many of the smaller rooms do not require the extra security. This is because we don't want to feel as though we are living in a fortress and seeing as though Ricon has never been attacked, we don't want to live in unnecessary fear. All of this is done purely as precaution," explained Tilly.

The children placed their hands on the machine and a blue laser extracted all the necessary information. At the same time a second laser came out from the side of the machine and scanned them from head to toe.

"Great! Now that's out of the way, we can move on to..." but before Tilly could finish her sentence, the door leading towards Zophia's office burst open and Tania flew backwards into the room landing hard on the floor.

"Get down and stay down!" Tilly yelled at the children as she ran towards Tania to see if she was ok.

The children did as they were told and dropped straight to the floor but kept their heads tilted up towards all the action.

As soon as Tilly had reached Tania, two tall menacing figures concealed by hooded black capes walked into the room.

"TYRIANS!" Tilly immediately opened her wings up and formed a shield to protect her body. She flew directly towards one of them. The Tyrian pulled out a long black staff and aimed it towards Tilly. A laser like beam shot out. Tilly quickly turned away from the beam, it bounced off one of her wings and hit the wall opposite, just missing the Tyrian it originated from. The force from the impact of the beam caused her to fall straight on to the floor.

By this point Tania had managed to get up off the ground and saw Tilly in a vulnerable situation. Both Tyrians were now heading towards her. Tania ran straight towards the one closest to her, jumped up into the air and performed a flying kick, knocking it off balance and enabling Tilly to get back onto her feet. They then turned their creators into glass-like swords.

The Tyrians used their staffs to defend themselves from the swords and get into a good position to shoot at the Riconians. All of a sudden one of the laser beams managed to knock the sword out of Tania's hand and it grabbed hold of her.

Its sheer strength was too much for Tania to fight against.

The children gasped in horror as it raised an arm and a sharp black spike appeared from the forearm section of its shiny black armour. It swung its arm towards Tania's stomach in an attempt to stab her. Tania managed to free herself from its grip, but as she did so, it sliced the top of her arm.

"OWWW!" Tania yelled.

"I'm so sorry," it replied, much to the surprise of the children until it morphed into Christopher.

Tilly along with the other Tyrian whom the children, by now, had realised was Appie, rushed over to Tania to see if she was ok.

The cut was deep and Tania was clearly in a lot of pain. Christopher quickly placed his hand close to the cut and using the creator healed it.

"I'm so sorry, I really didn't mean to do that," apologised Christopher again.

"No serious damage done, I'm ok now," said Tania.

"Are all of you ok?" Christopher asked the children.

"Well my heart is beating really fast but I think I should be ok," said Ilene. The others still in shock, nodded in agreement.

"We wanted to give you a taster of the training you are about to undergo and also familiarise you with the Tyrians. Appie and Christopher please could the both of you turn back into Tyrians so the children can have a closer look?" Tilly asked.

They did as she requested. As they pulled the hoods of the cape down, the children instinctively took a step back. They were disgusted and horrified by what they were seeing.

The Tyrian's eyes were twice the size of a human's but were red in colour without a hint of white and had no eyelids so they were permanently open. They had two small holes in their face where their noses should have been and sharp-jagged yellow and brown stained teeth. Their heads and faces were similar in appearance to a balding old man with wrinkled jaundiced skin. Their bodies were tall, around seven foot in height and quite muscular in appearance. They were dressed from head to toe in some kind of black body armour that could enable sharp black spikes to appear from various parts. The children also noticed their black staffs were similar in texture to their creators.

"This is what the Tyrians we have seen look like. The only Tyrian whose appearance we are unsure of is Master Tyler, their leader. From what we have been told, he is exactly the same in appearance except for the colour of his eyes which are black. Black like onyx, soul-less and pure evil," said Tilly, just as Harpz entered the room.

"Please allow me to introduce you all to Harpz, one of Zophia's main guards, and also one half of the greatest fighters the Riconians have ever had. Her other half being her sister Candace whom you will all meet later on," explained Tilly, bowing slightly, out of respect, and taking a few steps back to allow Harpz to take her place.

"Thank you for that glowing introduction."

"I would like to start by pointing out that your training here on Ricon will be very intense. A Riconian has to be able to take in and act on information fast. Both my sister and I are Zophia's main guards so at least one of us has to remain close to Zophia whilst she is here on Ricon, that's why we are not giving this talk together.

We are also the Heads of the Security Team here on Ricon. There are about thirty Riconians who are permanently based here as security… who knows, maybe one day you'll be part of that team.

Ok, for this part you may all have a seat," said Harpz, as she made six plastic chairs appear, for the children, in front of her. Four more seats appeared behind her, for the mentors to be seated on.

"We took a chance placing you in a group together as you have very different backgrounds and personalities, but after a few... well lets call them *incidents* during your training, you finally put your differences aside and showed us that you all have the qualities needed to become a Riconian and especially the most important one – strength!

I'm not just talking about physical strength, you don't need much of that with the creator around but what I am talking about is strength of mind. Consider the creator as extension to your mind, as that is exactly what it is. The creator not only enhances the power your brain already has, which on its own is incredible, but it also has its own unique powers, most of which you now know.

Some of the other qualities you have, and are essential as a Riconian, are courage, determination and respect. The only things we do not respect are the Tyrians but we do not hate them. Hatred will only make you weak and prevent you from focusing on the more important things. They have a job to do and so do we. However, they show us no mercy so we do exactly the same. When you fight them, attack them as if you are going to kill them.

Don't feel uncomfortable at thought of killing them, they don't die! They'll disappear in front of you and end up back on their planet, Tyron where they take a couple of weeks to recover and then get back to duty."

Harpz then touched her creator to make a chair appear in front of the children. She sat down on it so that she was eye-level with the children. She leant forwards and continued talking.

"I understand all of this is a lot to take in. And knowing that the Tyrians are our merciless enemies must be quite daunting. I'm not going to lie; they are very powerful, devious and evil but you cannot allow yourselves to be afraid of them.

You are capable of being just as powerful, and much smarter than them.

Tyrians, like us, are controlled by Higher Beings, but theirs are evil. All of their orders are passed on to them by their leader, Master Tyler. He has a role similar to Zophia as they are both our main contacts with the Higher Beings.

To our knowledge, Master Tyler has never left Tyron and as a result we don't know too much about him. This is a slight disadvantage as we are not too sure of exactly what he is capable of doing or his exact role on Tyron.

We are currently training an elite group of Riconians to go under cover as Tyrians to find out more about how they operate.

Zophia on the other hand likes to involve herself with events on Earth and on Ricon. She is also the person who has the final say in choosing the assignments we are given.

Riconian assignments are tough and involve a great amount of detective work. The only information we usually have about the subjects of our assignments is a name and location and not much after that. It will be up to you to establish why your subjects have been chosen by the Higher Beings and how the Tyrians are planning on sabotaging their lives.

Your main task is to prevent the Tyrians from getting close to the children or child you are protecting! Neither you, nor a Tyrian, can have control over a person's action. It's only their minds and ways of thinking that you can influence. The Tyrians will do whatever they can and cause events to happen in order to get what they want. You need to be on your guard constantly!

Tyrians, just like us, have the ability to easily change their appearance which makes our job on Earth, protecting our subjects, even more difficult. We can never be totally sure of knowing if we are interacting with a human or a disguised Tyrian. They also have the same dilemma as us but they have the advantage of being able to sense when a creator is being used. This means that when you are on Earth it is essential to use your creators cautiously and only when you are absolutely certain there isn't a Tyrian close by."

All of a sudden Harpz's attention was drawn to the pocket in her sash where the creator was. She took it out; it was vibrating and changing into different colours.

"Duty calls! I'm afraid I am needed elsewhere! Good luck! But you won't need much as you wouldn't have made it this far if you weren't capable of becoming a Riconian," she said, before disappearing out of the room.

Prashan twisted his body on the chair to face the mentors.

"Has she been called out to something serious?"

"I honestly doubt it! Candace and Harpz are always being called away and it is rarely for anything too serious," answered Tania.

"Well, we have some time to kill whilst waiting for Candace to arrive. As Harpz mentioned the assignments, I'd like to say that as your mentors it is our job to keep a close eye on you during your trainee assignment. In the same way we watched over you on the island, we will be observing you again. However, unlike the island, we have no control over what happens. If you or people around you are in danger, we will help. But should we need to do this, you will fail the assignment, return to your lives on Earth and your memories of the past few months will have been erased permanently," explained Tilly.

Kaia opened his mouth to say something to Tilly, but before the words could come out, the room went dark and a large three dimensional hologram of the creator appeared a few feet in front of them.

"You have impressed us greatly when learning to use the creator. There are, however, a few other uses for it you need to become familiar with. It can give you the ability to freeze time, although not for very long, only five seconds. It also transforms into the only weapons capable of defeating the Tyrians.

The ability to freeze time is very simple, hold your creators whilst saying the words 'freeze time' in your heads and everything around you will freeze. Be warned, it doesn't work here on Ricon and you cannot freeze any other Riconian. It will however freeze everyone on Earth and Tyrians," boomed a voice from hidden speakers.

The hologram then changed from the creator into the glass sword.

"This is the only weapon capable of penetrating through the Tyrian's armour. It's made out of a material caller verrine, the same material as the creator and Riconian wings. It's similar to glass as it is transparent and can be very sharp but it won't shatter as it has a flexible, rubber-like texture.

Transforming your creator into a sword is as easy as transforming it into any object but it will be your skills, as fighters, which determine how effectively you use your sword. Watch and closely observe the following fight sequences. All of these are based on various martial arts and sword fighting moves and techniques."

All of a sudden the hologram of the sword was replaced by a life-sized hologram of Harpz and Candace. The two figures began to demonstrate various fighting moves. They started off with basic punches, kicks and blocks through to more advanced open palmed attacks, followed by jumps and flying kicks. The moves then went from kicks and punches to the two figures throwing each other around and finally a sequence of moves using the swords.   The children sat in silence, concentrating hard.

Miella felt really uneasy, she hated fighting, and was worried about how she was going to cope with this part of the training. Kaia, on the other hand, loved playing computer games that involved fighting. He knew some of the moves already as he had acted them out at home, pretending he was fighting the enemies he had just defeated in the games.

As soon as the demonstration ended, the hologram disappeared and Candace appeared.

"Hi, I'm sure you can all guess who I am. I'm sorry for turning up late but my sister and I had to assist Zophia with an urgent matter.

The first rule of fighting as a Riconian Warrior is that we never attack. We only fight in defence. We never fight amongst ourselves, nor are we allowed to fight against humans. If a human tries to attack us then we freeze time, move out of their way and into a position where we can restrain their actions or make a quick exit, depending on the situation. We are the fighters that we are for one reason, and one reason alone... defeating the Tyrians! If they attack us then we fight.

You have all just seen a multitude of different moves and techniques. Having mastered the moves on their own, you will then be taught how to incorporate the use of your swords with them and against the Tyrians and their weapons.

As you all saw today, the Tyrians are tall, heavy and strong beings. This can be both an advantage and disadvantage. If they catch you off guard then their sheer strength alone can trap you and cause you to have an injury, as you saw happen to Tania. However their size and weight means they are unable to fly like us and are not as quick on their feet as we are.

They also have two types of weapons they are able to use against us.

The first that we will look at is the black spear, which is called a noilance. This shoots out an electric current which solidifies and penetrates our flesh as soon as it touches us.

At first you feel a sharp stabbing sensation travelling through your body which eventually leaves it feeling like it is on fire. Only another Riconian can help if you are attacked in this way as you are paralysed from the pain. When they pull the large needle-like object out, you will bleed but then they will heal you straight away.

From what we know there is nothing a Tyrian can do to kill us, however they certainly know how to inflict a tremendous amount of pain. If they are attacking you in this way then use your wings to shield you. The beam of current reflects off our wings and can sometimes, if you are lucky, bounce back onto the Tyrian on whom it has the exact same effect. If however it hits an object then the impact can often leave a hole or set it on fire, depending on the material.

During your trainee assignments we are more interested in seeing how well you can handle and deal with any situations that occur rather than your skills as a fighter. Those skills we will observe here first and only when we are completely happy with your abilities will we give you your first assignments.

It goes without saying, that your best form of self-defence as a trainee, and a Riconian, is to not allow your real identity to be discovered. However at times this cannot be helped.

The second weapon they use is the spike that appears out of their armour. They can control where on their bodies they want the spike to appear and although it is extremely sharp, it isn't very long so you have to be quite close in order for them to attack you in this way.

The spike contains a poison which enters your blood stream and directly attacks your mind. At first it causes you to start hallucinating, making you very paranoid and fearful. You will then fall into a coma and can take weeks, sometimes months to recover.

If you ever see a Riconian attacked like this, make sure you get to them as soon as you can and zel back on to Ricon immediately. They will then be cared for by Riconians who are specially trained in dealing with these situations.

The spike is the Tyrian's favourite choice of weapon on Earth as it sends you back to Ricon and out of their way so they can continue with their mission.

The best way to prevent yourself from being attacked by the spike is by chopping off their arms with your sword so they cannot grab hold of you. Then chop off their heads off. All it takes is one fast swoop with the sword. A sticky and smelly blue substance shoots out causing their body and head to disappear in front of you and return to Tyron to recover.

You now have the chance to practice those moves with your mentor. Zophia, my sister and I will monitor your progress and I will return as soon as I am satisfied that you are able to defend yourselves properly."

Candace then bowed at all of them and disappeared out of the room.

The children stood up and followed their mentors who by now had spaced themselves out in different parts of the hall.

"I can't do any of that stuff!" Miella remarked.

"Miella, just try it, you've nothing to lose by trying," said Appie

"I can't! I'm going to look silly!"

"Look around you, look at Kaia. Everyone else is trying, so why can't you?"

"I'm just not a fighting type of person. I love sports and ballet, but Kaia was the one who loved all that fighting stuff. I just can't do it!"

"Ok Miella, you say you did ballet... well pretend you are doing one of your ballet moves, one of those jumps but extend your leg half way through the jump as if you were doing a kick. Go on try it. Please, for me..." Appie said with a cheeky grin on his face.

"Ok, I'll at least give it a go," said Miella reluctantly. "Just don't laugh at me!"

Miella bent her knees, took a jump up and kicked out just like Appie told her.

"Well done!" said Appie.

"I can't believe I just did that," replied Miella, surprised by the result.

"Good! Now practice those moves with Kaia, pretend you two are fighting but without hurting each other. Spar with each other," said Appie.

… … …

Assignment

All the children and their mentors were gathered in the Grand Hall training, with the exception of Tilly. By now the children knew they were good fighters, and were thoroughly impressing their mentors by the ease in which they were demonstrating their new skills.

Candace appeared suddenly and they all stopped what they were doing.

"Congratulations! After four intensive months of training, Zophia, Harpz and I believe you are all now more than capable of defending yourselves successfully against the Tyrians, if necessary.

Tilly would like all of you to meet her at the bottom of the stairs, as she has some news for you."

The children immediately zeled out of the room and gathered where Tilly had asked. Their mentors had also disappeared.

Another Riconian walked past them and smiled. Kaia smiled back wondering how he would feel like when it was him walking past a group of trainees.

Tilly, Appie, Christopher and Tania suddenly appeared in front of them.

"We have some good news for you. An assignment has been found, so without any further delay, follow us to one of the workstations!" Tilly said.

The excited children followed their mentors to the fourth floor where the corridor walls were covered in mirrored verrine panels. Tilly stood in front of one of the panels and placed both her hands on it. A door suddenly appeared at the entrance of the corridor and closed them all in. The whole area they were in became very dark except for a blue laser-like light that appeared from the bottom of the new door and travelled to the top scanning everyone.

"What's happening?" Conor asked.

"Don't worry! This is just for security purposes. The laser is simply identifying you," replied Tania.

The lights came back on suddenly and everyone blinked a couple of times so their eyes could adjust to the change. The mirrored panels around them slowly started to disappear into the ground, transforming the area they were in, into one large room. The main part of the room had a very homely and inviting feel to it. There were a couple of large sofas facing a large flat screen monitor and the warm lighting added an extra level of comfort.

One corner of the room was sectioned off by verrine walls. Within this area were several computers, monitors and other bits of machinery that children had never encountered. On the opposite side of the room were six beds and a closed door positioned not too far away.

"I noticed you looking at the door Prashan. It leads to a room where we'll be staying through out your assignment and this room here is where all of you will be based," explained Christopher.

"Get comfortable so we can explain all," he added, pointing to the sofas. Tilly positioned herself in front of the screen, facing the children. The other mentors, Christopher, Appie and Tania stood behind the children.

"This is the final part of your training, and the most important, as you are all aware that failure results in returning back to Earth."

Tilly then turned to face the monitor on which a picture of two children appeared on the screen. "These two boys are the subjects of your assignment. Alex is on the right, and on the left is Ian," said Tilly.

Miella wondered what was so special about the two of them that would have the Tyrians chasing after them. They both looked quite tall for teenagers. Alex's hair was neatly braided in rows and his complexion was a caramel colour, quite similar to hers and Kaia's. As the image on the screen zoomed in on their faces, Miella noticed he had very long eyelashes emphasising his large brown eyes. The other boy, Ian, had quite a milky complexion, dark brown hair and green eyes.

"All we know about these two is that they live in London, and are very talented athletes. You may have seen Alex before as his mother is the famous Hollywood actress Tamara, and his father is her manager. They are based in London but as his parents rarely spend much time there, Alex is left on his alone for most of the year. Ian lives alone with his mother. Neither of them have any siblings. They go to different schools but are best friends having met through athletics.

Whatever it is that the Tyrians are planning is going to happen soon. If they succeed then these children's lives will be lost. As they are still on their summer holidays, neither of them will be at school, instead they will be spending a lot of time at the track, training.

The best way to approach this, we believe, would be for two or three of you to base yourselves in the room over there with all the complicated looking equipment... the Control Room. By all means you're free to leave the Control Room to have a break here or sleep on the beds over in the corner but we wouldn't advise zeling into your bedrooms whilst on an assignment because you could be needed at anytime. Situations could arise and you might only have minutes if not seconds to make a decision. At least one person should be there at all times. Do not be put off by all the equipment, it's all very easy to use.

The other three who decide to be in the heart of the action, would be better off not interfering with what is happening in the Control Room. Focus solely on what is happening with your subjects, Alex and Ian in this case, as well as finding out who the Tyrians are and putting a stop to whatever their plans are!

We would suggest you take it in turns so that there is at least one who remains behind. This is so that if an emergency does occur, the third person watching all of the action from Ricon will be able to make a better judgement on what to do.

Whoever remains here would also need to act as a messenger in case anyone in the Control Room needs to let someone on Earth know something urgently, if it is not safe to use the creator to make contact.

I'll now give you ten minutes to decide amongst yourselves who would be best suited to the different posts and once you have decided, let me know. Any questions?"

"I have one," Prashan said, with his arm slightly raised.

"When we get to Earth, won't our subjects find it strange that these new people - us - have turned up and are interfering in their lives?"

"Good question and its something I forgot to point out earlier on! You will appear 'in disguise' so to speak, as new people in these children's lives in order to fit in easily. You need to have your story straight at all times! You can change your appearance as and when you wish but don't slip up by forgetting key pieces of information which could lead to a Tyrian discovering you. Any more questions?" Tilly asked.

No one responded.

"Ok, your ten minutes start now," she said, whilst walking over to the Control Room with the other mentors, to give the children some privacy.

"Well does anyone have any idea of what they would like to do?" Conor asked.

"I think I'd be much better suited to the Control Room," replied Ilene

"Me too," said Prashan

"I wouldn't mind being on Earth," said Patricia

"I think it'd be quite cool to be an undercover agent, I'd like to be on Earth too," said Miella

"Looks like it's down to the two of us Kaia, any preferences?" Conor asked.

"Not really, maybe I should stick with Miella. You decide! I really don't mind."

"Well, I guess it makes sense for you and Miella to stay together so I'll settle for the Control Room," replied Conor.

Kaia turned around to face the Control Room and waved to get their mentors' attention. Appie popped his head around the door.

"We've made our decisions," said Kaia.

"So quickly? I'm impressed!" Appie replied.

All four mentors then walked out of the Control Room towards the children.

"Ok so Miella, Patricia and I will be going to Earth and the other three will be based in the Control Room."

"Well if you are sure, Conor, Prashan and Ilene follow me and Christopher into the Control Room where we'll show you how to use the equipment," said Tania.

The five of them then disappeared into the Control Room leaving Tilly, Appie, Kaia, Miella and Patricia in the main room.

"We now need to figure out some kind of plan of action," said Tilly.

"Are you sure you don't have any more information on them?"

"Not much more, sorry Patricia! All we know is that they are fifteen years old and very good at athletics," explained Appie.

"But how are we supposed to get close to them on Earth if we have no idea of where they are going to be? We can only zel from one place to another when we know what the place looks like. I know you said they are in London but London is a big place," said Miella.

"Don't worry too much about that! Zophia will decide that when she sends you to Earth. Once you are aware of your surroundings there shouldn't be any problems with you zeling back and forth. Zophia will also decide on what you look like when you first appear in their lives. You can then morph yourselves as you wish in order to complete the assignments. So... now on to the next question... who's going down first and who's staying behind?" Tilly asked.

"I think the cousins should!" Patricia said with a crafty smile.

"Cheeky!" Miella replied. "That's fine, we'll go first!"

"Ok! But don't think you have the easy way out Patricia! You'll have to really observe what is happening on Earth and be ready and prepared to jump in or take over when necessary. Well, if you're ready to get started, I'll go and inform Zophia," said Tilly.

"I am ready, how about you Kaia?" Miella asked.

"More than ready, let's go!"

"That's really good to hear! I'll inform Zophia, in the meantime prepare yourselves," said Tilly, before zeling out of the room.

"I'll go and inform the others in the Control Room about what is happening," said Appie.

About forty-five minutes passed by. Christopher, Appie and Tania were now standing around and talking to each other in front of the main screen. Ilene was seated on the sofa talking to Miella and Patricia. Conor and Prashan were in the Control Room ensuring they were comfortable using the equipment. Kaia zeled back into the room, having returned to his room to prepare for the task and sat down on the sofa next to Patricia, Miella and Ilene. Tilly then entered, followed within seconds by Candace and Zophia.

As soon as Prashan and Conor saw that Zophia was present they joined everyone else.

"Tilly has informed me that you are all ready to start your first assignment. I have been given constant updates on your progress and must say, I am very impressed at how fast and how well you are all adapting to life on Ricon and the challenges you have faced so far.

This however will be the toughest challenge so far!

Miella and Kaia, if you are ready, come over to me and I'll send you down to Earth. If everyone could get to their positions, we can start this assignment. I wish all of you the very best," said Zophia.

Ilene, Prashan and Conor stood up and walked over to the Control Room, followed by the mentors who headed towards their Observation Room. Appie stopped and turned around to face the children. The other mentors automatically did the same.

"Good luck," he said, and the other mentors then wished them the same.

Kaia and Miella stood nervously in front of Zophia. Miella looked at Candace. She smiled back and winked reassuringly.

"Ready?" Zophia asked.

They nodded at her.

Zophia placed one hand on each of their shoulders and muttered something. They then disappeared out of the room.

II

Kaia looked around, "Oh no! How could Zophia have done this to me?"

He tried to find Miella was but it was difficult to spot her amongst the crowd, and as the noise coming from them was deafening, there was no way for him to hear her, if she was trying to call out to him.

Kaia turned to his right and saw Alex in the lane next to him. Ian was in the lane to his left.

Miella stood in the crowd shouting at Kaia but knowing it was all in vain because of the noise. She then caught a glimpse of her reflection in the mirror of a female spectator who was in front of her, re-applying her lipstick.

The peroxide blond goatee-beard against her much darker complexion and bald head was certainly not what she was expecting to see staring back at her. She heard the race being announced over the tannoy and as soon as she heard Alex's name a feeling of dread over came her.

"Oh, that's strange! In lane five we have a new entry for this hundred metres sprint and for some bizarre reason I can't seem to find his name amongst my notes! Apologies and good luck kid," said the race commentator, sounding very puzzled.

Kaia raised his hand and waved nervously.

Miella looked at Kaia feeling really sorry for him but also finding the situation quite amusing. She knew Kaia was never a good sprinter and always tried to come up with excuses to avoid participating in his school's sports day.

She watched as he set himself up in the starting blocks. He still looked the same as before but Zophia had given him a much more athletic body. If there was one thing Kaia would be happy about, it would be his new physique.

The starter pistol sounded off in the background.

Miella really didn't want to see the outcome because she was cringing for Kaia. The race was obviously over in a matter of seconds. Alex won and Ian came second. As Miella had expected, Kaia came last. He wasn't too far behind but there was no way that he was fast enough to be racing with the others.

Kaia limped towards Alex with his hand stretched out.

"Well done," he said, trying to shake Alex's hand.

"Are you alright there? You look like you're in pain!" Alex said, slightly concerned by Kaia's fake limp and fake grimace.

"Yeah, I think so, it's an old injury just playing up," said Kaia lying through his teeth, but doing so quite convincingly.

"Well you're walking on it so you should be ok but get it checked out by the medics just to be on the safe side... oh this is my boy Ian, by the way," Alex said, as Ian appeared next to them, placed his arm around Alex's neck and patted him on the back with the other hand, congratulating him for winning the race. Alex reciprocated by giving him a hug back.

"Ian meet... hold up, what's your name as I have no idea," said Alex.

"Kaia."

"Kaia, I'm Alex and this is my best friend, on and off the track, Ian."

Kaia shook hands with Ian.

"What are your plans for tonight?" Alex asked Kaia.

"Nothing planned so far," replied Kaia.

"Well I'm having a party at my place. Come along if you want! Bring your girl or a friend along too. I'll be expecting to see you there. Do you know where Wembleston is?" asked Alex.

"Yeah, I think so," replied Kaia.

"Well then you have no excuse to not be at my party. I live at Hill Mansion on Hill Road, which is past Wembleston Village towards the Common. We'll see you there. The party kicks off at nine tonight," said Alex.

The two of them then walked over to a tall, tanned, blond man who looked in his late-thirties, and a group of girls standing right by him.

"That was a fantastic race you ran there – not," said a deep masculine voice from behind him. Kaia turned around and a look of disbelief appeared on his face.

"What a poor performance! We really need to work on your technique," said Miella with a straight face, then bursting into laughter having seen the look of confusion on Kaia's face.

"Kaia it's me!"

"Miella?" Kaia questioned in a state of disbelief.

"Wow, Zophia really went all out on you," he said, laughing along with his cousin.

"I saw you talking to the real stars of the track, what were they saying?"

"Well actually, they invited me to Alex's house for a party tonight," said Kaia in a rather smug tone of voice.

"Excellent work, did he give you an address?"

"Yeah, it's an easy one, Hill Mansion, Hill Road, Wembleston. Remember that until we can find a pen to write it down with."

"Ok, so what do we do now?" Miella asked.

"Returning home, I guess! But we need to find somewhere well away from these people before doing so."

They two then walked away from the track and out of the main gate. The track was situated in the middle of a large park so Kaia and Miella walked on for about ten minutes, deeper into the park, hid behind some bushes and zeled back to Ricon.

As soon as they arrived back, Patricia, Conor, Prashan and Ilene started applauding Kaia.

"Oh well done Kaia! The way you ran in that race was something else!" Patricia laughed.

"Kaia! We had no idea you were so talented, at fake limping that is!" joked Conor.

"Very, very, funny guys. Absolutely hilarious!" Kaia replied sarcastically.

Miella stood next to Kaia, laughing as well.

"Thanks Mimi, I would have expected a little loyalty from you."

"I'm sorry but you should have seen yourself, it was funny!"

"Go ahead and have your fun at my expense but I don't have time to listen to any of it as I have to get ready for a party tonight and where will all of you be? Oh yeah, silly me! How could I forget? STUCK HERE! See ya!" Kaia said as he walked towards the bathroom.

Miella walked over to the sofa and sat down. Patricia sat next her as Conor, Ilene and Prashan walked back into the Control Room.

"About the party, Patricia, I think it would be a good idea for you to go there as Kaia's friend."

"Are you sure you don't want to go?"

"Yes, I'm sure plus I think this would be a good opportunity for you to get into the action... and it's a party... what could possibly go wrong? Have fun!"

"Thanks!" Patricia replied excitedly, running off to get ready.

III

"Kaia, landing on my backside in this dress was not what I had in mind. You really need to improve on your landing skills. It's not a good way to impress your date!"

"Firstly, this is not a date! Secondly, get up off the grass quickly before you draw attention to yourself," replied Kaia sharply.

"Well this is going to be a fun night if you remain in that kind of mood. NOT!" Patricia snapped back at him.

"Patricia, I'm sorry! I get really nervous using the creator under normal circumstances but with it being dark here and the two of us alone in the middle of this massive park...Well, just imagine how you would feel if we bumped into a Tyrian now," apologised Kaia.

"I didn't think about it like that. Point taken! Let's get out of here as quickly as we can. How are we going to get to Alex's house from here?"

"We jump into a black cab, easy!" Kaia said, as his saw one approach from the main road, and started running towards it.

Patricia and Kaia stopped the cab at the gate of Alex's mansion.

"Wow, check this place out! I have never before seen anything like it," remarked Patricia.

"I guess it is fairly impressive," replied Kaia.

There was a high wall rimmed with barbed wire along the top, a large iron-grill gate surrounding a beautiful Tudor styled mansion, with a long gravelled driveway and beautifully maintained lawn, trees and flowers paving the way to the front door.

Alex was at the front door, welcoming his guests. Kaia and Patricia stepped out of the cab and walked towards him, and Ian, who had now also appeared.

Kaia relaxed a little as he drew closer. He could hear the music blaring out of the house and was finally looking forward to enjoying himself and having some fun.

"Hi Kaia, good to see you! Did you find the place ok?" Ian enquired.

"No problems at all. We just got a cab down from the station. This is my good friend Patricia, " said Kaia.

"Hello Patricia, nice to meet you," said Alex shaking her hand then introduced Ian.

All of a sudden the music stopped playing, there was a loud crash followed by shouts and screams. A boy with blonde hair came out of a room and ran towards them.

"Alex, a massive fight has just broken out, come quick!"

Alex and Ian ran behind him. Kaia and Patricia looked at each other and then instinctively followed the others.

Alex's front room was in chaos! Furniture and food were being thrown about. Some people were trying to stop the fight whilst others were aggravating the situation.

"STOP!" Alex screamed in vain.

"What do we do?" Patricia asked panicking.

"I don't know! We could easily sort out this mess with the help of you know what but we can't risk it," replied Kaia helplessly.

"I know..." replied Patricia. She then spotted sprinklers on the ceiling. "Kaia look for some matches or a lighter!"

He looked at her, confused at first, but then had an idea of what she was planning when he saw where her eyes were focused.

"Nice one, Patricia!" Kaia replied, as he looked around the room whilst trying to avoid the fracas. "I've found a lighter!"

"Great, I've found some matches!" Patricia shouted back above all the noise from the other side of the room. She saw a magazine lying on a little coffee table, stood on the table, lit the magazine and held it up to the ceiling.

Kaia did the same with a newspaper he found lying around.

The smoke from both burning objects reached the smoke detectors. An alarm sounded off, followed by water shooting out from the sprinklers.

Patricia's plan had worked. Everyone started to run out of the room to avoid getting wet.

"GET OUT!!!! EVERYONE, JUST GET OUT OF MY HOUSE!" Alex screamed.

Ian switched off the sprinklers and then made his way to the front door to ensure people were leaving.

The only ones remaining in the room were Alex, Kaia, Patricia and two other girls.

The room was a mess! Glass was shattered all over the place, damp furniture knocked over, food smeared all over the walls and carpet, in addition to puddles and stains from all the spilt drinks.

"I think this is my fault, I'm sorry!" said a pretty dark haired girl.

"What do you mean, it's your fault?" Alex demanded sounding confused and angry.

"Please don't be mad at me, baby," she begged.

"Bettina, what did you do? Look at this room! My parents are going to kill me! How is this your fault?"

"Well Natalie told me she overheard a girl saying that she was going to take you away from me and that I wouldn't be able to do a thing about it. So I confronted her and she got aggressive. She had her face up so close to mine yelling at me that I pushed her and maybe a bit too hard because she fell down... but... by this time a group of people were crowding around us and then her brother and his mates started yelling at me... and before I knew what was going on everyone around us was fighting. Alex I am really, really sorry..." she said sobbing.

Alex looked at her blankly.

"Get out," he said in a very disappointed tone.

"JUST LEAVE! I can't deal with you right now... go home."

"Alex, please don't be mad at her," said the brunette girl.

"You too Natalie, just go," he replied, not even looking at her.

"But Alex..."

"Come on, now's not the time," said Natalie, grabbing Bettina by the arm and walking out of the room towards the front door.

"I'll call you!" Bettina shouted out before leaving.

Alex didn't reply he just stared coldly at them as they left.

"Would you like us to give you a hand tidying up?" Kaia asked.

"I can't ask you to do that, I've only just met you," replied Alex, shaking his head in disbelief, as he scanned the mess.

"We don't mind," replied Patricia.

"You know I'm not going anywhere either," Ian said, trying to reassure him.

"Thanks, it'd be good if you could."

They then set about tidying up. Kaia and Patricia were tempted quite a few times to use the creator to speed up the tasks but didn't as they were not too sure as to whether there was anyone else in the house. As soon they had finished, the four of them threw themselves on the sofas, exhausted from all their hard work.

"I don't know how to thank all of you! Ian, you know I would have done the same for you, but Kaia and Patricia, I just don't know what to say except... thanks, I guess!"

"No problem! It's nearly morning, we really should make our way home," replied Patricia.

"You are both welcome to stay over, there's plenty of room," offered Alex.

"As tempting as that sounds, I think it's better if I head back and get some sleep. I have some tough training ahead of me.

How about the two of you? Won't you be training?" Kaia asked.

"Yeah we'll be at the track today around three. That's the time that Jon told us to be there, right Alex?"

"Yeah three," replied Alex, half asleep.

"If you want, you could join us, and we can get some dinner after, my treat! Please make sure you come along too, Patricia."

"I'll be there, thanks!"

"Sounds like a plan," yawned Kaia

"I think it's time we left otherwise I have a feeling I'll have to carry someone out of here," Patricia said, looking at Kaia.

Alex dragged himself up out of his seat and headed towards the front door with the two of them following behind. Poor Ian was so exhausted that he had fallen asleep on the sofa.

Kaia, Patricia and Alex said their goodbyes and waited for Alex to shut the door before deciding it would be safe enough to zel back to Ricon from behind a tall tree at the bottom of Alex's driveway.

They arrived on Ricon exhausted, and found Miella still awake waiting for them.

"Well that turned out to be the party of the year!"

"Don't remind me Mimi! I'm shattered and off to bed. Please wake me up when it's time to go back down," Kaia said walking straight to the section of the room with all the beds in it.

Patricia sat down next to Miella.

"Aren't you tired Patricia?"

"A bit, but I thought I'd keep you company here for a little while."

"That's kind of you but Alex and Ian are both fast asleep so they'll be ok. We're both tired maybe we should also get some sleep as well," suggested Miella.

"What if something happens?"

"If it does, one of the guys in the Control Room will wake us up, but I doubt there'll be any real problems," replied Miella.

"I guess it would be a good idea to get some sleep. I'll come with you to the Control Room to ask them to wake us up if anything significant happens."

Miella and Patricia walked over to the Control Room, had a little chat with Ilene and Prashan and then went to sleep.

IV

"Miella, wake up!" Ilene said, gently shaking her by the shoulder.

Miella opened her eyes.

"I've tried to wake Kaia up but he just won't move!"

Miella turned around to look at Kaia. He was fast asleep, breathing quite heavily.

"Ian and Alex are down by the track waiting for him."

"Leave him be, I'll go down and pretend to be Kaia. Just give me a couple of minutes to sort myself out and I'll meet you in the main room."

"Ok," replied Ilene as she walked off to wait for Miella.

Miella transformed herself into Kaia but the more athletic one. She was really tempted to wake Kaia up so he would get a fright at waking up and seeing his double, but she stopped herself from doing so as she knew she didn't really have time to waste.

She went into the main room where Ilene was waiting for her and zeled down close to some trees not too far away from the track.

As she made her way towards the track, she spotted Ian and Alex with the older man she had seen on the first day.

"Hi Kaia, glad you could make it," said Alex.

"We thought you would be too tired," added Ian

"I am! But I can't let that get in the way of training," Miella replied.

"I like your attitude kid! I'm Alex and Ian's coach, Jon. All I have heard from these two is that they were up all night playing computer games and now they are too tired to train. It's just not a good enough excuse! In fact it's an awful excuse so they are being pushed twice as hard as I normally would. How about you? Are you ready to join them?"

"Erm, I think I had better warm up a bit before I get into any serious training. I'm already recovering from one injury so I don't want to aggravate it or make it worse."

She knew she was a bit better at running than Kaia but definitely not on the same level as Alex and Ian. The only way she would be able to pass off being an athlete would be if she used the creator. She decided it should be ok to use it, if she had to, but only if no one else turned up. She was obviously safe around Alex and Ian and figured she should be safe around Jon.

Miella was so heavily engrossed in her thoughts that she didn't hear Jon shouting at her.

"KAIA!"

"Huh? Oh sorry, I was miles away," replied Miella.

"I'd say you've warmed up enough, are you ready to show us your stuff?" Jon asked.

"Just give me a couple more minutes and I'll be there, giving both Alex and Ian a run for their money," she replied, cursing herself silently for what she had just said.

She sat on the grass and continued stretching in an attempt to stall time and think up any other options.

"Alex, your performance has been awful lately!" said Jon

"But he won the race the other day and nearly beat his personal best," exclaimed Ian, defending his friend.

"No one was talking to you! However, now that you have my attention, you're not doing much better! At this rate neither of you are going to qualify for the Junior Championships!"

"But I have been doing really well... I was right behind Alex in the last race," replied Ian.

"I have just said Alex was not doing well so you coming second means you're worse! When you race Kaia now, I want to see both of you really push yourselves!"

Listening to Jon, Miella was glad to have never been an athlete and if she had been, he would have been the last person she'd want to train her!

"Kaia, are you ready mate?" Alex asked.

"I think so…"

"Great let's get going!"

Miella was dreading this moment so much! She really didn't want to use the creator but knew it was the only way she'd be able to pass herself off as a sprinter.

"KAIA! KAIA! Stop right there young man!" A loud voice shouted out from behind her.

All four of them turned around.

Miella smiled. Right in front of her, walking towards them, was Kaia's coach. The person she had first appeared as.

"Kaia you know you are not allowed to train until your leg has healed properly. Thankfully I had Patricia's telephone number. Yours is always switched off!"

Miella knew straight away by that comment that it was Patricia disguised as her coach.

"Now listen Kaia! I know you are in a hurry to get back into training but I am your coach for a reason so you have to start listening to what I say," Patricia said, trying hard to not laugh at the look of relief on Miella's face.

"Hello, I take it you are Kaia's coach. I'm Alex and Ian's coach, Jon," he said, with his arm out stretched for her to shake.

"Hello… Del. Well, Derrick really, but everyone calls me Del. Pleased to meet you but I'm afraid it has to brief as Kaia and I should get going. I have to have some serious words with this young man about not listening to me," she replied, worried that Jon might start baffling her with some technical running terms, if she remained.

"No problem, I'll be having a similar chat with these two lads as well. Sometimes it's like trying to get blood out of a stone, especially when you know they can do so much better with a little more effort!"

"Hmm, I know exactly what you mean," lied Patricia. "Kaia, let's go!"

"Coming! Sorry guys! I should have mentioned I was still struggling with my injury before. That's why I was taking so long with my warm up and stretches."

"That's ok, are you still up for dinner tonight?" Alex asked.

"Definitely!"

"Great! Meet us by the statues outside Wembleston Station in about four hours time. Just at the top of the steps... oh and don't forget to bring Patricia!"

"I won't! See you later Alex, you too Ian!" Miella said and then walked off with Patricia.

"Ohh, did you hear that? He wanted Kaia to make sure that you're there. I think he likes you!" Miella teased.

"Stop trying to wind me up or I won't come to your rescue ever again! He's only inviting me because I helped last night!"

"Ok, if you say so! By the way, thanks for saving me. I thought I was going to have to use the creator to run against the two of them."

"So you *were* planning on doing that! Ilene thought so, as you kept on touching your pocket, which is why she woke me up. Are you insane? For all you know Jon could be a Tyrian!"

"I don't think he is! He's their coach and must have been for years... surely that would rule out him as a Tyrian," explained Miella.

"Miella you don't know anything for certain! It's too risky to make guesses before using the creator. We know they are at work here otherwise we wouldn't be here... Please, think things through a little more carefully before you make any decisions about using the creator," pleaded Patricia.

"You're right! I am so sorry! I just didn't want to look like a fool in front of them... I feel so stupid now!"

"It's cool! You didn't use it so there is no point stressing over it now. Let's just get on with this task and succeed, you know what will happen if we don't!"

Returning to Ricon, they found Kaia and Ilene seated on the couch waiting for them.

"Ilene, thanks a lot, you really saved me out there," Miella said before hugging her.

"Wow, I'm really good looking aren't I?" Kaia said, staring at Miella.

"What are you on about?" Miella replied, then realising she was still disguised as him. She immediately changed back to herself and playfully hit Kaia on the top of his head. She then sat down in between Kaia and Ilene and placed her head on his shoulder.

"What's wrong?" Kaia asked.

"I still feel bad for nearly using the creator."

"Well you didn't use it and you now know better so there's no point dwelling on it. We still have a job to do so focus on that and not on what might have been."

"Patricia said pretty much the same thing. I guess the two of you are right! I still can't figure out why we have been asked to protect them, they both seem to know what they want and are training hard to do it. I can't see how the Tyrians can get to them," said Miella.

"Neither can I," added Patricia from the sofa next to theirs.

"Well, all the more reason why we have to be extra vigilant and aware of what is happening at all times.

Anyway, I need to get back into the Control Room, take over from Conor and keep Prashan company. Some of you have a dinner to get ready for and one of you has more of a reason to glam themselves up, hey Patricia?" Ilene teased as she stood up and walked towards the Control Room.

"NOT FUNNY!" Patricia shouted back in jest as Ilene walked away.

"Ilene has a point. We really do need to pay more attention… don't the both of you think you should start getting ready for your dinner?" Miella asked.

"I don't know if I can wait that long Miella, I'm kind of hungry now," said Patricia.

"Yeah, me too," admitted Kaia.

"Well why don't the three of us have something now and then you two can go and have a drink or desert or something with the others," suggested Miella.

"Best idea I have heard all day," said Kaia as he used his creator to make a feast appear in front of the three of them. After they had eaten, Kaia and Patricia got ready and zeled back to Earth.

V

Kaia and Patricia stood by the statue, on time, waiting for Alex and Ian. Ten minutes passed by, and then another fifteen, yet neither had turned up.

"Ok, we'll give them another fifteen minutes and get back to find out what's happened." As soon as Kaia had said that, he saw Ian and Alex walking towards them. Alex was on crutches with his foot heavily bandaged.

"What happened?" Patricia asked really concerned.

"Just after you left, Jon got… well how can I put it… quite intensive, shall we say, with the training and I felt my ankle pull but he made me carry on saying that it was just a little twinge.

I carried on but the pain just got too much for me so I went to the hospital. They said it was a fairly bad muscle strain and I'd have to keep off it for a week or two. I can't believe this has happened! The Junior Championships are in just under a month. This is going to put me out of training for at least two weeks," said Alex, almost in tears. "Anyway let's go and sit down somewhere," he continued, trying to change the subject so he wouldn't cry in front of them.

"Erm, well actually, Patricia and I were starving earlier so we have already had something to eat – sorry," said Kaia, feeling slightly guilty.

"No problem, I know a place we can go to, it's an American style diner and it's just around the corner. Ian and I are hungry so we'll grab something there and you guys should try the awesome milkshakes in there," suggested Alex.

"Perfect, let's go!" Kaia said.

The four of them made their way to the diner and sat down in one of the booths.

"You're crazy for coming out to meet us, shouldn't you be resting at home?" Patricia asked.

"That is exactly what I have been trying to tell him," said Ian.

"I'm sure all of you are right but the thing is, I know that if I stayed at home I would just be moping around. And as my parents aren't due back for a few more weeks, I would rather be out trying to have some fun than be indoors upset and alone."

"I guess I can't really argue with that! By the way, what's with your coach? He really didn't appear to be doing you any favours, in fact if it was me he was training I would probably have quit by now. He just zaps any fun out of it!"

Ian chuckled, "Trust me Kaia, sometimes it is hard for me to keep my mouth shut. I feel like cursing him so badly but he has a reputation as one of the best coaches around. He trains some of the adults in the actual Olympic Team, so the fact that he is willing to train us as well is a privilege. Our last coach was much nicer but he had some family problems so went back home to America about six months ago," explained Ian.

"So Jon has only been your coach for a couple of months?" Patricia asked.

"Yep, I think this month will be the fourth month of training under him. Alex's parents heard from a friend of theirs that he was the best in the business and they pulled in a whole heap of favours to get him to train us.

He's not cheap either! If Alex's parents didn't pay for me then there would be no way my mother could afford to… like I said, sometimes I am just dying to say something back to him but I know it would only work against me so I keep my mouth shut," admitted Ian.

Patricia and Kaia exchanged worried looks having heard this information.

"Oh no, here comes trouble," said Alex as he glanced and saw Bettina walk in with Natalie and three other guys. She walked straight over to Alex.

"You didn't tell me you were going to be here," she said bluntly.

"I didn't think I needed to!"

"Oh, don't tell me you are still mad at me about the party? I told you it wasn't my fault. Get over it already! Anyway, who are your new friends? Are you going to bother to introduce me to them or do I have to do it myself?" Bettina asked, not even bothering to mention his heavily bandaged leg, sticking out from under the table.

"You really are something else at times, introduce yourself!"

"Hi, I'm Kaia, this is my friend Patricia," Kaia said, trying to diffuse the tension.

"Hi, I'm Bettina. I'm supposed to be Alex's girlfriend and if anyone cares we'll be sitting over there," she said, pointing at seats a few tables down from where they were. She then turned around and walked away with Natalie. The other three boys followed behind.

"Excuse me for a moment." Alex said standing up and then hobbled over to them on his crutches.

"Sorry! I really don't know why Alex wastes his time with her. We've something to discuss quickly... I feel really rude for leaving you both but it shouldn't take too long," Ian said before joining the others.

"Wow, I'm so glad Bettina isn't my girlfriend," said Kaia

"What a cow!" Patricia said, with a look of real disgust on her face.

"I she's definitely different... oh well! She's not someone for us to worry about anyway. I saw the expression you made when Ian was talking about their coach, are you thinking what I am thinking?" Kaia asked.

"I guess so! He would be the most obvious suspect so far! We really need to keep a close eye on him. It's going to be hard now that Alex isn't training. Our only way is through Ian but how?"

"That's something we all need to figure out..." Patricia and Kaia were suddenly distracted by some shouting coming over from the area where Alex and Ian were seated in.

"NEVER! There is no way you're dragging us into that, just forget it!" Ian shouted as he walked away from the booth and stormed out.

Alex picked up his crutches and tried to catch up with Ian. As he passed Kaia and Patricia, he dug into his pockets, pulled out a twenty pound note and slapped it onto the table.

"I'm really sorry about this! If you are free, I'll be home tomorrow. Come over around eleven, if not then I understand! Again...sorry," he said as he carried on after Ian, shortly followed by Bettina, Natalie and the others.

Kaia and Patricia turned their heads toward the front of the diner to see the heated discussion continuing outside.

"We need to be there with them," Patricia exclaimed.

"You're right," agreed Kaia as he grabbed his jacket and headed towards the doors. But by the time they had paid for their drinks, the argument had ended. Alex and Ian walked off in one direction, and Bettina and the others headed off in another.

"Maybe we should just leave them alone for now and try and get some information out of them tomorrow. Hopefully the others back home would have been able to pick up on what was going on."

"Let's hope so as we really need to know what's taking place," replied Patricia.

"I agree," replied Kaia. They then set about finding a safe place to zel back to Ricon.

VI

"Wow, what an eventful day," Miella said excitedly, upon their return.

"I know! I have so many thoughts and theories buzzing around in my head at the moment, it's crazy," said Patricia.

"Me too," agreed Kaia.

"Coach Jon has just become the no1 suspect in my opinion," exclaimed Prashan.

"Mine too! We have to be very careful around him! We managed to pull up some information on him from the computers and it would appear that he is who Alex and Ian say, and has an excellent reputation as a coach. I just don't understand how from his behaviour today," admitted Conor.

"Well, I guess it's because of these Junior Championships that we're here. I'd imagine it'd be quite an achievement if they win and no doubt lead on to bigger and better things. But clearly their minds are distracted by other things. That's what you three need to work on," said Prashan.

"You're right… but Alex has been injured, how is he going to train?"

"Err hello Kaia! Have you forgotten about this little toy? We can use it to heal subjects!" Miella held up her creator.

"Of course! Apart from zeling back and forth from Ricon and Earth, I hadn't really thought about the creator! I guess I was too busy thinking about Tyrians," admitted Kaia slightly embarrassed.

"Well it looks like one of you is going to have to give his ankle a little massage, hey Patricia?" Conor said teasing her.

"Eugh gross! There is no way I am touching anyone's foot and I've had enough of all the jokes about Alex. Ok, I'll admit it, he's cute but I'm seriously not interested in him," replied Patricia.

"I'm sorry! I was just kidding, I couldn't resist," said Conor.

"Well, who's going to sort out his ankle, I'm not planning on doing any of that business," said Kaia in a very blunt tone.

"Well then, I guess it would have to be up to Coach Del, feet, ankles, legs, hands whatever, Coach Del can fix all problems," joked Miella.

"Excellent idea! That way Coach Del could also have a few words of encouragement for both Alex and Ian." Prashan added.

"I like the way you think my friend! I like it a lot! Perhaps Coach Del could even offer to help them with their training?" Conor suggested, with a crafty smile.

"I don't know the first thing about athletics and training people," said Miella.

"That really shouldn't be a problem, you could help them to train in a secluded area with no one else around and use the creator to give them a little more encouragement if needed," said Conor.

"Good point and it sounds like an excellent plan! We'll have to try to work it into the conversation tomorrow when we meet up with them," said Patricia.

Ilene popped her head out of the Control Room, "No one has mentioned his girlfriend Bettina. I think we need to look out for her!"

"Yeah, there is something about Bettina that just doesn't make sense. Did anyone catch on to what all the arguing was about?" Kaia asked.

They all shook their heads and either said or mumbled a "No".

"That whole incident is really bugging me," said Patricia.

"And me... I think we all want to know what exactly was going on there. We'll have to try and find out about that too," said Miella.

"Roll on tomorrow, I can't wait," said Kaia.

VII

Kaia and Patricia walked up to the gates of Alex's house.

"I hope he's in a better mood today," said Patricia

"Me too! I think Ian was in a much worse state than Alex yesterday but whatever was happening we need to get to the bottom of it," replied Kaia, as he pressed on the buzzer by the gates.

"Oh hi... come on in," said Alex's voice over the speakers. Patricia and Kaia walked up the path to find Alex waiting for them by the door.

"I am so sorry about yesterday, all I seem to be doing since meeting the both of you is apologising!"

They followed him to the living room where Ian was seated.

"Hello Kaia, hi Patricia, look I am really sorry about last night."

"Ha ha... I was just saying that ever since we met them, I've been apologising non-stop, and now you do the same too," laughed Alex, as he hobbled to a sofa, sat down and then dropped his crutches on the floor.

"Please stop, it's fine! Is everything ok with you guys? If there is anything we can do to help or you know, if you want to talk about anything, then please do! We don't know your friends so we can give you advice or an opinion that is

141

completely impartial," said Patricia, noticing a sly smile of approval on Kaia's face.

"I wish you could sort this one out but its best if you stay completely out of this, best for you that is! Thanks for the offer." Ian said with a worried expression on his face, trying to force a smile.

"Well, you know where we are if you ever change your mind. So are you off to train now?" Patricia asked, as Ian was dressed in his tracksuit.

"No, I wish! That's something else going all horribly wrong! Jon called me this morning. He said he has a lot going on in his personal life at the moment needs some time to figure a few things out.

He feels awful for pushing Alex so hard and with him now being injured so close to such a major competition, as a result of training, means he really isn't doing his job properly.

He's given me the telephone number of a friend of his who also coaches, but from what I have heard, he really isn't very good. Everything just seems to be turning into one great big nightmare!" Ian said, shaking his head in disappointment.

"Looks like we're both pretty much out of the race now and it's such a horrible feeling because I'm sure I would have won at least a silver medal and Ian a gold without a doubt!" Alex said, slumping further into his seat.

"This was supposed to be my way out, get me away from being around those idiots from last night and make my life better. My life is... was, all about athletics. All that has gone now," continued Ian.

"Ok, stop right there! Feeling sorry for yourself won't help! The competition is still on in four weeks, right?" Patricia asked.

"Right!"

"Ok! Well, I am sure Del wouldn't mind coaching you two... Oh and as for Alex's ankle, let Del have a look at it. He's really into alternative therapy or something like that but whatever it is it's usually very effective. Kaia strained one of the muscles on his thigh and after Del did something to it the pain went away immediately, didn't it Kaia?" Patricia asked, sounding so convincing that even Kaia started to believe her.

"It was much better after he looked at it. You have to train with Del and I'll get him to have a look at your ankle too. I'm sure he won't mind... it can't hurt to ask can it?" replied Kaia.

"Are you sure you don't mind? I mean both you and Alex will be competing against each other in the same race, doesn't that bother you?" Ian asked.

"No! If I am to be honest, you should know I don't really like competing. My mum was a really good runner when she was younger. I'm only doing it because she wants me to. Don't get me wrong, I enjoy running but I hate big competitions!"

"So what do you guys think? Are you up for giving it a chance?" Patricia asked.

Alex and Ian both looked at each other, slightly unsure.

"I suppose it can't hurt to try." Ian replied.

"Alex how about you?" Kaia asked.

"I honestly doubt he'd be able to sort out my ankle," replied Alex, "... then again, why not? I guess I have nothing to lose!"

"Excellent!" replied Kaia almost jumping out of his seat with excitement as their plan was working out so well.

"I'll give Del a call now! I was due to have a training session later on today around two o'clock. I am sure he won't mind you two coming along!"

"Oh... I'm afraid we can't do today... we have to meet up with some people around that time," replied Alex.

"NO, NO! We don't! Two is fine! In fact two's perfect. I'm not going to do it Alex... we are not doing it," said Ian, suddenly sounding really angry.

"Didn't you hear what was said? We have no choice!"

"Look, Alex it's not you they are concerned with. They're just dragging you into this because of me. Arghh! I am sorry I ever introduced you to any of them, especially Bettina! This is my problem. I'll deal with it, not you," replied Ian abruptly.

"Ian, you know what'll happen if we don't go through with it! We have no choice! As for Bettina, I only met her through you. You had no part to play in what happened after, and yes, things have changed but I'll deal with her when the time is right."

"Alex, we have a competition to think about and that comes before them. Kaia two o'clock today will be fine. Thanks!" Ian said, turning his back on Alex.

"But...."

"No buts! That's it! My mind's made up!"

"Are you sure we can't help?" Patricia asked, both confused and intrigued by their conversation.

"Sorry! I forgot you two were there! Look, I really appreciate the help with the training and stuff but this is something you would both be much better off staying out of. Ok... so two o'clock right? Well it's coming up to half twelve, maybe we should get going," suggested Ian.

"Er... yeah, sure! Let me give Del a call, I'll just pop outside for a minute." When Kaia got to the door he turned around, looked at Patricia and discreetly signalled for her to meet him in the hallway.

Patricia waited for about a minute and made her excuses to go to the bathroom, and joined Kaia.

"What's wrong?" Patricia whispered.

"I'm worried about them missing whatever it is they're supposed to be doing at two o'clock. Do you think we should say that Del will only be ready at four so we can follow them to see what is going on or do you think that it would be best if we went training, at least we know they're safe with us?"

"I was thinking about that too, we really need to know what is going on and how serious it is! Oh, I don't know either! I suppose the best thing would be for you to go training. I'll make my excuses and head back to discuss this with the others. As soon as we have a plan, I'll turn up at the track." said Patricia.

"Yeah, I think keeping them away from whatever it is that is bothering them, until we know exactly what is going on would be best. Listen, I'll go back into the room, you follow me in about a minute or two so it doesn't look like we were talking about them," said Kaia.

"Ok," replied Patricia.

Kaia then entered the room and as he did so, he interrupted a whispered, yet heated discussion between Alex and Ian, they both seemed very worked up.

"Kaia, we are going to have to cancel, please apologise to your coach," said Alex.

"No we are not! I am going training with Kaia if you want to come then come. If not then stay here! Come on Kaia, if you guys are ready then let's go," said Ian, just as Patricia entered the room.

"Hold on, let's all go, I'm coming," Alex said reluctantly as he reached for his crutches and stood up.

"I'll leave you guys to it, I've made some plans with some friends and they live in the opposite direction," said Patricia.

"That's right, I forgot you had mentioned that to me earlier on," Kaia said, trying to add some credibility to her story.

"Oh, ok! I doubt watching us run up and down the track would have been very interesting for you anyway. Hope you have fun with your friends," said Ian as four of them reached the gate and then said their goodbyes.

Patricia started to head off in the opposite direction but then hid behind a wall and making sure no one was close by, returned to Ricon.

VIII

"Help! My head is just spinning," exclaimed Patricia, as she collapsed on the sofa next to Miella and Prashan.

"Trust me, we are just as confused as you are," replied Prashan.

"Miella you'd better get ready to leave as they have arrived at the park and are making their way towards the track!" Ilene shouted, from the Control Room.

"Thanks! I'm just trying to prepare myself mentally. I don't know how I'm going to pull this one off! Acting like I actually know something about training people to run is going to be hard," Miella said unenthusiastically.

"Miella, snap out of it! You know you will be fine. Use the creator when you need to, as long as it's just the three of you and no one else around," said Prashan

"Argh, don't mind me, ranting away! I'll figure something out when I get down there," said Miella

"Listen, if I were you, I'd do focus solely on their training and nothing else. Fix Alex's leg and then get them both running and excited about the competition so their minds are off whatever else is going on. In the meantime we'll try to figure out what we should do next... you'd better get going," said Prashan.

"Ok, thanks for the advice, I'll see you guys later," said Miella as she transformed herself into Del and zeled herself back to the park.

IX

"Well, well, well! These must be the two young men you were telling me about Kaia!" Coach Del said walking up to them.

Kaia smiled at his cousin. "Del, I'd like to properly introduce you to Alex and Ian." Miella greeted them with a firm handshake.

"So Alex, I see you have some strange running equipment attached to your arms. I'm not too sure those would be allowed to accompany you in any of the races! I guess we'll have to do something about getting rid of them. Kaia and Ian why don't both of you do some stretches and warm up whilst I see what I can do about this injury."

"You seem very confident that you can do something about my ankle," said Alex.

"I've treated many sprains and had the person running straight after. I don't see why you would be any different. Take a seat on the grass and take your trainer off."

Alex did as he was told. Miella then crouched down and squatted right by his feet.

"Ok... before you start doing anything I'd like to know exactly how you're going to make my ankle better," exclaimed Alex, very nervously.

Miella looked at him straight in the eyes.

"First of all, *RELAX*," she said trying to buy some time so she could get a story straight in her mind.

"Ok this is a combination of techniques I've learnt from my travels around Asia," she bluffed.

Alex looked at her, still feeling nervous.

"Please, just relax! It doesn't hurt! You might feel a little heat running along the injured muscle but then you'll be fit to run, right away. Now let me have a look," she said as she took hold of his foot and pretended to examine it. She then stuck her hand in her pocket and touched her creator. She looked around the park... the coast was clear. She changed the creator into a cloth, pulled it out and placed it on his ankle.

"Ok, I need you to close your eyes and relax completely."

Alex did as he was told.

Miella looked around the park again to ensure they were alone and put the creator into use by gently massaging Alex's leg with the cloth.

"I can feel something happening," he said excitedly.

"Shussh, just relax!" She moved the cloth away.

"Ok, now gently move your ankle and tell me if it's still painful."

"No! It doesn't hurt anymore," he exclaimed in surprise.

"Ok, stand up slowly and tell me how it feels when you put some pressure on it. Take a couple of steps," advised Miella.

"No nothing... I can't feel any pain at all," he said, almost crying with delight.

"Ian, come over here!" Alex yelled.

Ian jogged towards them, Kaia followed behind.

"My ankle's healed! I think I'll be ok for the competition!"

"How did you manage to do that?" Ian asked, surprised by how easily Alex was now moving around.

"The people who taught me how to heal have sworn me to secrecy. Kaia should never have told you about my ability to heal these minor ailments but I can understand why he did.

You two, on the other hand, are not allowed to repeat what has just happened. Not under any circumstances! Just be grateful for the ability to be able to run again, is that understood?"

Alex and Ian nodded in agreement.

"One other thing, this is more for your benefit than mine, do not mention to your coach that I'm helping you. I don't want any trouble from him."

Miella was still convinced Jon was a Tyrian. She didn't believe the story about him having personal problems. Alex's injury, and disappeared and so suddenly after, seemed too fishy for her liking.

"Ok I want all three of you to get ready for a proper run. Alex, have you warmed up enough?"

He nodded.

"Good! Now line up here and get in to your starting positions. Don't make this a race to see who is the fastest between the three of you, make it a race to beat your own personal bests. Imagine the finishing line and being the first through it, imagine how it will feel to look at the clock and see that you have not only won the race but also set a new personal best. It feels good just imagining it right?"

Alex and Ian, smiling, nodded their heads in agreement.

"Well now stop imagining it and make it happen! ON YOUR MARKS... GET SET... GO!" yelled Miella, holding a stop watch in each hand.

As soon as the race was over, Miella read out the times to Alex, Ian and made one up for Kaia, who respectively came first, second and third.

"Can you repeat that time please?"Alex asked with a look of disbelief and surprise.

"Mine too," asked Ian, sounding just as curious whilst trying to catch his breath.

"Sure! In fact here... have a look for yourselves," said Miella, showing them the stopwatches.

"NO WAY! I *have* beaten my personal best!" yelled Alex, spinning around and punching the air in delight.

"ME TOO!" Ian exclaimed.

Kaia stepped over to Miella and whispered, "Mimi... do you think it was such a good idea using the creator and getting the two of them so excited and worked up, so soon?"

"Kaia, I didn't use it! They did this on their own. I did absolutely nothing to help. I am just as surprised as they are. It is *really* good news though!"

"Wow!" Kaia was stuck for words.

"Exactly!" replied Miella

The training session continued for about an hour with Alex and Ian consistently performing well.

X

After training had ended, Alex invited Kaia back to his place for dinner. Approaching the gates to his house, Kaia noticed a group of five dodgy looking individuals standing outside.

"No way! What the hell are they doing here?" Ian said sounding worried.

"I have no idea... quick let's turn around," said Alex.

"Too late. They've already seen us, just keep walking... don't let them think they intimidate you," instructed Ian taking the lead.

"Well, well! Look at what we have here! We had a meeting a couple of hours ago, forget that did you? Surely you're not stupid enough to try to avoid me, are you? Who's the new muppet with you?" asked a tall and slightly chubby, blonde man Kaia had never seen before.

"We had a training session and you leave him and Alex out of this. This is between us," replied Ian.

"Who do you think you're giving orders too? You've just gone and got your new mate involved as well now, nice one! Anyway, you're in luck today! I'm in a pretty good mood so I'm going to give you the benefit of the doubt and think the reason you didn't turn up was because you forgot to... and not because you were avoiding me, right?" He said pushing his face up so close to Ian's, that their noses were practically touching. He then gritted his teeth and snarled, "Don't ever keep me waiting! You know *exactly* who you are dealing with! That alone should scare you enough into doing as you are told!

Tomorrow morning the three of you'll be meeting me here at ten with a plan of how we're going to go ahead with all of this, or else!"

He then turned around to the group of boys behind him, "Come on lads, let's go. These guys have a long night ahead of them, best we leave them to it!"

As he passed Alex he stopped, "Rich boy! I heard you were barely able to walk yesterday... miraculous recovery, hey? It'd be such a shame if something was to happen to both of your legs, wouldn't be able to do much running then, now would you? Let's just hope that never happens... to any of you!" he said, eyeing up Ian, Kaia and Alex. He then got into his car, followed by the rest of his group, and drove off.

As soon as he had turned the corner and was no longer in sight, Ian threw his sports bag on the floor and started kicking it furiously. "Why is he doing this to me? Why won't he leave me alone?"

"Shhh, stop shouting and come on into the house," said Alex, placing his hand on his distressed friend's shoulder.

"At the very least you owe Kaia an explanation... are you alright mate?" Alex asked Kaia.

"Fine... confused but fine!" Kaia replied.

"Don't worry, once we're indoors, we'll fill you in," said Alex.

They all walked into the front room.

"I'm so mad that they're trying to drag you into this nonsense. Jerome never used to be this bad!"

"Don't tell me you two were friends!" Kaia exclaimed in disbelief

"No, I was friends with his younger brother Fabian. We all lived in the same area... Arrghh, this is such a long story! Basically, my mum used to manage the local Post Office and I'd sometimes help. He now wants me to break in and rob the Post Office because I know where everything.

Mum no longer works there as she came into a bit of money and we moved out of the area but I kept going to the same school. I started to get some grief from some of the other kids because they were jealous of the money we inherited.

Everyone who knew Jerome was scared of him so when his brother stuck up for me, the other kids pretty much left me alone. Jerome went to prison, not long after we moved. His mum then decided that she'd had enough of everything that was going on and didn't want Fabian to turn out like his brother and also left the area. Jerome was released from prison recently and now thinks I owe him something because his brother helped me out and as a result his family moved," Ian explained in despair.

Kaia just sat in silence.

"Hey, don't worry, I'll think up some way of sorting out this mess," said Ian.

"No, that wasn't what was going through my mind! This guy is a complete idiot! I don't understand how he can think that you being his brother's friend would mean you now owe him something," said Kaia.

"I know! But… well… the way that he sees it is that Fabian got into a few… erm, let's just call them 'situations' by defending me. So now Jerome thinks that if Fabian never helped me out, their mother would never have had a reason to move away."

"That's just stupid! How can he think like that?"

"Well, you saw him today, does he seem like an intelligent or reasonable type of person to you?" asked Alex.

"No! Anyway why's Alex involved?" asked Kaia.

"Because it would take more than one person to do the job and obviously he doesn't want to get caught up or be associated with any of this. He would be sent straight back to jail if he did," replied Alex.

"What do you think would happen if you don't go through with all of this?"

"Quite honestly I really don't want to think about it! Let's just say that threatening to break our legs would only be for starters… he really is a nasty piece of work!" Ian replied.

"Well, why don't you go to the police?"

"And say what? He would only deny everything and then come after us. He's not playing around! I have thought of every option Kaia... every option! I have to do this, there is no other way but I am not taking either of you two down with me," said Ian.

"Let's not go there again! I've already told you there's no way you're doing this alone, I'm involved... even Bettina said I had to go along with you otherwise Jerome wouldn't be happy," said Alex.

"Ok, listen! There is no way *any* of us are going to get involved with this stuff. You two have so much going for you with the athletics. You can't let such a major opportunity go because of this guy," said Kaia.

"Well what else can I do?" Ian asked.

"What if I said I can get him off your back? Leave it to me and you'll never deal with him again. The only thing I ask in return is that you concentrate on the competition coming up as you have already put so much effort and time into it... don't let that be wasted."

"Why are you so concerned about us and what can you do to help?" Ian asked, unsure of how to take Kaia's offer.

"Well, I told you the main reason I train is because of my mother. I know how much she regrets not giving it her all because she is trying to live it all through me and I would hate to see that happen to anyone else," lied Kaia, very convincingly.

"Fair enough, I suppose... but how are you going to deal with Jerome?" Ian asked.

"I'm not too sure just yet, but let's just say I have quite a few friends in high places who'll help. Don't worry, there won't be any repercussions with the police or risk of Jerome implicating either of you with whatever happens. I promise! Please, just trust me!"

"I'm not too sure," replied Ian.

"Answer one question... the pair of you. What's more important to you at the moment, Jerome or the competition?"

"The competition, of course!"

"Same here," replied Alex giving Kaia a very strange look.

"Fine, then you concentrate on that and I'll sort Jerome out. It'll all work out."

"Kaia, I am sure you mean well, but all of this seems a bit weird. I mean why would you go out of your way to help us?" Alex asked.

"I'm also involved now, remember?"

"I guess, but still, I really don't know," replied Alex, shaking his head and shrugging his shoulders.

"I promise the situation will be sorted and neither of you'll be affected. Please trust me," replied Kaia.

"Ok, we'll trust you," replied Ian, still uncertain, but willing to take a chance.

"Thank you," replied Kaia, sighing with relief.

"I'm going to head off right now. Don't worry about turning up tomorrow to meet Jerome. Just meet Del for your training session. I'll see myself out," said Kaia.

"HEY KAIA!" shouted Alex, as he opened the door of the living room.

"Yes?"

"Thanks, thanks a lot! I still don't know why you are doing this but it's the only option we have at the moment so I guess it's worth a try," said Alex.

Kaia then walked out of the house feeling like his head was ready to burst as he had so much running around in it.

… … …

PLAN

I

Miella, Patricia, Conor, Ilene and Prashan hadn't even noticed Kaia arriving back on Ricon as they were all standing by the Control Room, in deep conversation.

"What's going on?" Kaia asked.

"We're just trying to figure out a plan to help Alex and Ian. So far, Conor has come up with the best," said Miella.

"Well what is it?"

"I was thinking that tomorrow morning we could go down and meet Jerome pretending to be Ian and Alex and stand up to him ourselves. He would back off then. I am sure of it!" answered Conor.

"Erm, I doubt that would work. From what I have heard about this guy, he is bad news and I doubt that standing up to him would put him off," replied Kaia.

"I think I have an idea," said Prashan quietly.

"Sure, go ahead, what is it? Ilene asked.

"One of us should turn up in disguise and hang around the meeting point. When Alex, Kaia and Ian don't show up, Jerome and his sidekicks won't be happy and will plan and plot what they are going to do next.... at least this way we'll know what they are thinking of doing to them, should this next part not go to plan. We need to get Jerome on his own and somehow warn him off! I think turning into a Tyrian, in front of him should do the trick! If it doesn't, then I don't know what will!"

"Prashan you are a genius!" Ilene exclaimed excitedly.

"This could work, although we may have two problems. The first being that we'll need to use the creator, so should a Tyrian be close by, it'll know where we are, and the second being the need to get Jerome on his own. He might try and plan to do something straight away with the rest of his gang," said Miella

"Well in that case we have to make sure Alex and Ian are somewhere safe. Not at either of their homes or places they would usually hang out. Maybe they should spend the day training," suggested Prashan

"That should work but what if the Tyrians try to attack?" Patricia asked.

"That's the only real issue here. The chances of any of Jerome's little sidekicks being a Tyrian is minimal and I honestly doubt Jerome is one himself as he's been in Ian's life for too long," replied Prashan

"Even if they are, we know how to defeat them so that shouldn't be a problem," remarked Conor.

"Now we just need to sort out exactly what is happening, who's doing what and how to put it into action!" Miella said.

II

Miella was the first to wake up the following morning. She looked around the room trying hard to ignore the butterflies that at were going crazy in her stomach. She wondered how the others could sleep so soundly with such an eventful day ahead of them. Miella didn't have the patience to wait around so set about waking everyone up. As soon as they were ready, they gathered in the main area.

"Well, I guess the time has finally come! As I'm the first person to kick this plan into action, wish me luck," said Patricia as she morphed into Coach Del, and zeled onto Earth.

Patricia landed behind a tree in an alley by Alex's house. She had a good look around as she knew it was risky landing there in daylight. Luckily for her there wasn't anyone close by, and anyone living in the nearest house was still too far to notice what she was about to do.

She held her creator in both hands and closed her eyes to help her concentrate as her nerves were getting the better of her.

A car appeared in front of her. She got into the car and started the engine up. She made sure the set up of the inside of the car was the same as a go-kart but managed to make it look as close to the inside of a normal car as she could so the children wouldn't be suspicious. As the only to one to have any experience behind a steering wheel, even if it was just that of a go-kart, they had decided that she would be best to meet up with the kids, disguised as Coach Del.

Nervously, she reversed and then pulled the car out of the spot it had been in. As soon as she started driving, she relaxed as the creator made driving really easy. She just had to concentrate on directing the car to where she wanted it to go.

Arriving at Alex's house, she pressed the intercom.

"Hello, who is this?" asked the voice on the other end

"It's Coach Del, who is that? Alex?"

"No it's Ian."

"Are you ready to go? Is Kaia with you by any chance?"

"No he isn't and we weren't expecting you either," replied Ian.

"What? Why not? Open the gates so I can drive up and talk to you once I am parked inside."

Ian opened the gate for Patricia to drive up, she then got out of the car and walked up to Ian and a half-asleep Alex at the front door.

"Lads, why are you not ready?"

"We didn't know you were coming here," said Alex.

"I don't know what that boy Kaia is playing at. He called me up late last night to tell me he cannot make training today but asked if I could pick you two up earlier than planned," said Patricia.

"Why would you pick us up? The track is just down the road, we can walk there as usual... and Kaia never mentioned any of this," replied Ian.

"He told me he would call one of you as soon as he had put the phone down to me. Anyway forget about Kaia for now, I'll deal with him when I next see him! I have decided to take you to train at a proper stadium on the otherside of London as I believe it would be a good experience for you. We'll be gone the whole day, so hurry up and get changed as there isn't time to waste. It's already 9:15!"

Alex and Ian, not having any reason to doubt her, did exactly as they were told.

III

Kaia zeled down to Earth as himself and into the park where he knew Jerome would be waiting. He landed by some bushes, close to the main road yet far enough to not be seen by anyone. He then closed his eyes and imagined himself as an old man with a wrinkly bald head, thick glasses, and tatty clothes under a just as tatty looking full length grey rain coat and changed his creator into a walking stick.

As he made his way towards the meeting place, he passed through a little make-shift gravel car park where he spotted Jerome's car.

An unplanned idea popped into his head.

The night before they had all agreed that if Jerome tried to drive off, having realised that the boys were not turning up, then Kaia would use the creator to make a car and follow him. Despite agreeing, Kaia didn't feel too comfortable with that idea.

He walked closer towards the car, looking at the front and rear tyres closest to him. Making sure no one was nearby, he then pointed the walking stick at them and they suddenly started to deflate. He then strategically placed broken glass around the tyres to make it look like it they had been slashed by the glass.

As he looked up, feeling rather pleased with himself, he noticed a group of people in the distance. He was quite sure it was Jerome and the rest of his gang making their way towards the car park. Kaia decided to have a seat on a wooden bench by the entrance of the car park.

He sat on the bench, placed his walking stick on the ground between his legs, and lent forward on to it, keeping his head faced down towards the ground.

As the group of people got closer, their voices became louder but Kaia couldn't quite make out what they were saying.

He raised his head slightly, just enough to see exactly who was approaching him. Jerome was present, along with him were two other males and to Kaia's surprise, Bettina and her friend Natalie. As they approached the car park entrance, their voices were now completely audible.

"Jerome, calm down! I'm sure there's a good reason for them not turning up. They might even be late, you only waited five minutes! They're probably on their way or might even be there now waiting for you... tell him Bettina!" said Natalie.

"I don't know what to say, I can't speak for them," she replied.

"Shut up Nat! Five minutes late, is five minutes too long! Who do they think they are dealing with here? No one and I repeat NO ONE makes me wait for them! Julian, call for back up as we'll be paying Alex a little house call. I'm sure they'll be hiding there, and if not, then I guess we'll be having a little house party of our own until he arrives. Tell the others to wait around the corner until I get there!"

He was just about to dial but then stopped and mumbled, "Boss, look at that!"

"What the heck is going on today? There is no way this glass was here earlier on. NO WAY!" Jerome yelled, as he kicked the flat rear tyre in anger. "Oi... old man! Who did this to my car? You must have seen something!"

Unsure of what to do, Kaia pretended he didn't hear the question.

"Oi granddad... you ignoring me? Who did this to my car? I know you saw something, don't make me beat it out of you!" shouted Jerome.

He approached Kaia and raised his hand in the air with the intention of punching or hitting him, Natalie quickly grabbed hold of it.

"This old fool ain't worth it! He's probably too old to remember anything at all," she said, trying to calm him down.

"Arghh, you guys stay here and sort this mess out. I'm going home. Jools, get my car sorted and then drive it over to mine. We'll call the others and sort those three out... once and for all!" Jerome shouted and threw his car keys hard on the floor. He then walked out of the car park and headed towards the exit.

"Jerome, wait! I'll come back with you," Natalie shouted.

"Stay the hell away from me today... I don't have time nor the patience for you! Go home... both of you idiots... just go!" Jerome yelled at Natalie and Bettina.

Kaia remained seated for a few more seconds as he tried to figure out what to do next. He now had the perfect opportunity to get Jerome on his own and scare him, as planned. He stood up slowly and started to walk towards the park's exit. Aware of his audience, Kaia tried his hardest to impersonate an old man walking, but he also knew he had to somehow catch up with Jerome. As soon as Kaia reached the exit, he turned around to see if they were still watching him and was relieved to see they had their backs to him, dealing with the car.

Kaia decided it was now safe enough to speed up in order to catch up with Jerome. At first, he thought he had lost sight of Jerome, but spotted his blue jacket. With Jerome in sight, Kaia decided to remain a safe distance away until he was certain it was just the two of them alone. Jerome then made a quick turn into an alley way. Kaia couldn't believe how well the plan was working out and started to run in order to catch up with him. As he turned the corner to enter the alley way, Jerome instinctively turned around.

"You... what do you think you are playing at? I should have dealt with you properly earlier when I had the chance!"

He placed his left hand on the collar of Kaia's raincoat and grabbed hold of it, then raising his right hand he swung a punch at Kaia.

Kaia took hold of his fist in mid-air and pulled it down sharply. He then grabbed Jerome by the neck and lifted him off the floor.

"I have a message for you," said Kaia, transforming into a Tyrian. "Stay away from Alex and Ian!" he threatened, now in full disguise and with a menacing voice.

From the look of horror and fear on Jerome's face, he knew that the plan had worked.

Kaia noticed Jerome's eyes shifting from him to look at something behind him. As Kaia released the grip he had on Jerome's neck, Jerome yelled, "Natalie... run, get the police! Quick, get out of here!"

Kaia turned around expecting Natalie to do just that but instead of running away, she walked towards him, with a slightly puzzled look on her face.

"Go away Nat, RUN!" shouted Jerome

Natalie stared blankly at him and continued to walk until she was directly in front of Jerome. She then turned herself into his double and mimicking his voice, repeated the words he had said to her earlier on,

"Stay the hell away from me today. I don't have the time or the patience for you!"

Jerome's complexion turned paper white and his eyes opened wide with horror.

Natalie then picked him up and threw him hard against the wall. His back took the brunt of the force of his body's weight and he slid down, hitting the ground hard. Throughout his ordeal, Jerome's eyes were fixed on his body double, until it turned into a Tyrian and he then fainted.

"So little Riconian, is this how you are now trying to defeat us, by turning into us? Pathetic!"

With his heart racing Kaia quickly changed back to himself. The Tyrian took hold of his spear, aimed it towards Kaia and fired. Kaia jumped out of its way but his nerves and fear were getting the better of him making him unable to use the creator properly. For every step the Tyrian took towards Kaia, Kaia took two petrified steps backing away.

The Tyrian clearly able to see Kaia's fear used it to an advantage by walking faster towards him.

Suddenly the Tyrian jerked forwards towards Kaia screaming out in pain, and dropped to his knees. Kaia then saw Miella standing behind him with the verrine sword in her hands.

"Oh Mimi, thank you so much! I don't know what happened to me. Do you think you knocked him out?" Kaia asked, as the Tyrian lay motionless on the floor.

"I'm not too sure," replied Miella, as she cautiously walked over towards it with the sword in her hand. All of a sudden the Tyrian grabbed hold of her leg with one arm and raised the other so that a spike appeared out of its armour, but before it could hurt her, Kaia chopped that arm off in one quick swoop and then immediately sliced its head off. Just as their mentors had described a horribly smelly blue goo-like liquid shot out from its neck and dissolved the rest of its body.

"Are you ok?" Kaia asked.

"Fine, thanks for saving me!"

"I think it would be fair to say we both saved each other just then," Kaia panted.

"Do you think he is seriously hurt?" Miella asked, looking over at Jerome who was still lying on the floor.

"No, he's just had the fright of his life and maybe a few bruises, but apart from that I'm sure he'll be ok!"

"We can't leave him here like this! Do you think he got the message to leave Alex and Ian alone?"

"Only one way to find out," said Kaia, turning back into a Tyrian and then walking towards Jerome. Miella decided to turn herself into one as well. Kaia gently tapped Jerome on the cheek, to wake him up.

"Wuh?" said Jerome still dazed. Coming to his senses, he froze in horror as he looked up to see two Tyrians facing him.

"What do you want from me?" he asked, trembling with fear.

"We want you to leave Alex and Ian alone, change your ways and leave London! Move back home to be with your mother and brother, start a new life... in fact do whatever you want but just make sure you leave Alex and Ian alone!" Miella ordered.

Jerome looked blankly at her.

"Do you understand what we are saying?"

Jerome nodded his head.

"Good! Now get up and get out of here. Don't ever tell anyone what happened here. We'll find you if you do and I'll leave the rest to your imagination... do you understand?" Kaia asked.

Jerome nodded his head again and stood up.

"GET OUT OF HERE!" Miella yelled.

Without a second to lose, Jerome turned away from her and sprinted out of the alley way.

"I'd say he's got the message, wouldn't you?" Miella said, laughing.

"Definitely!" Kaia replied, also chuckling.

"Let's get back before someone else comes along," Miella suggested.

They both returned to Ricon to receive a warm welcome from the other trainees.

... ...

Race

The day of the big race had finally arrived for Alex and Ian. Kaia stood next to them in the changing room whilst Miella, disguised as Coach Del, gave them a few last minute tips.

Ian's two hundred meter race was before the one hundred meter event Alex was running in. There was an hour left to go before Ian's race and Alex's was scheduled to take place fifteen minutes after.

The four of them had grown really close since the incident with the Tyrian and Jerome. Ian heard news that Jerome had returned home suddenly. He knew it was as a result of something Kaia had done but as promised, neither he nor Alex had ever asked any questions regarding the matter.

There was a lot of media coverage for the race as Alex's parents had flown back from their Hollywood film set to watch their son in action. Due to all of the hype surrounding his parents, the race organisers decided it would be a good idea for Alex and Ian to be separated from the other athletes, not only for their own safety and security, but also so the other athletes would not be distracted by any journalists or photographers trying to sneak in.

There was a knock on the door.

Miella opened it and was surprised to see their old coach, Jon, in front of her.

"Hello... I was wondering if it would be possible to see the boys for a couple of minutes?" he asked nervously.

Miella looked at Alex and Ian for some kind of answer.

Ian shrugged his shoulders and then looked over at Alex for some kind of response.

"I guess that should be ok," replied Alex.

Jon walked in looking very anxious and unsettled.

"So how are the two of you? Oh... congratulations for getting this far!"

Miella couldn't help but stare at Jon as there was something about him turning up that made her feel very uneasy.

"We're fine! Ready and excited about our races!" Alex replied.

"Indeed! I have absolutely no doubt in my mind that you will win!" Jon turned to Miella and Kaia. "If I remember correctly you said your name was Del, right?"

"Correct!" Miella replied bluntly.

He held his hand out for Miella to shake it, which she did, but begrudgingly.

"And I haven't forgotten you, young man... Kaia wasn't it?" He asked, shaking his hand as well.

"I was wondering if I could ask the both of you to give us, say, ten minutes alone? I'd really like to have a private word with the boys," Jon explained.

"No! Sorry! As their coach, I am afraid I can't allow you to do that. "

"Please, it really would be just a few minutes! I need to explain what happened to me and why I had to stop training them," said Jon almost pleading.

"Can't you do that after the race?" Miella asked trying her best to get rid of him.

"It's fine Del! A few minutes shouldn't hurt," replied Alex.

"Yeah, we'll be fine!" Ian added.

"Ok, but only if you are both sure!" Miella said before she and Kaia unwillingly left the room and walked down the corridor.

"I really don't feel comfortable leaving them alone with him Kaia. What if he's another *T*?" Miella asked, not wanting to say the word Tyrian out aloud.

"I'm going back," she said, turning around suddenly.

Kaia grabbed hold of her arm.

"Mimi, don't! Leave them alone, you'll look a complete fool if you are wrong. We'll wait here, close by, in case anything happens."

Miella reluctantly agreed.

II

The atmosphere in the room was tense.   Jon stood in silence, with both his hands rigid in the pockets of his navy blue sports top.   Alex and Ian patiently waited for him to say something.

"Well you wanted to talk to us so the least you could do is say something," Ian said, after a few uncomfortable minutes.

Jon looked up at him with tears in his eyes.

"Sorry, this is really hard... I don't know if I am..."

"If you are what...?" Ian asked as he stood up and walked over to Jon.   He placed a hand on his shoulder to comfort him.

Jon looked at Ian's hand and grabbing it, pulled Ian close to him.   Ian was now facing Alex with his back firmly held against Jon's chest.   Jon had placed his left arm over Ian's left shoulder, locking tightly onto him.

"I am really sorry but there is no other way," he whispered into Ian's ear as he pulled out a knife from his jacket pocket with his right hand and held the blade against Ian's thigh.

"What do you think you are doing?" Alex shouted out really loud.

"Shut up!   Do exactly as I tell you and neither of you will get hurt," Jon shouted back.

All of a sudden Coach Del and Kaia burst into the room.

"I knew you were up to no good!" Miella shouted as she charged straight towards Jon, having heard all of the shouting.

"Stay where you are and he won't get hurt!" Jon commanded.

"Oh come on, we know exactly who you are, just drop the knife and deal with me!" Miella ordered.

"What are you on about?"

At that very moment a young boy who resembled Jon burst into the room and shouted, "Dad, what is going on?"

"Marc, go away I am doing this for you!"

"Dad this is crazy, you have been acting weird for weeks and now I know why!   Please put the knife down, don't do this!"

"I'm not going to hurt him son, I just want to keep him here long enough so he misses the race and then you'll be the one who wins," sobbed Jon

"Dad, I know I won't win against Ian this time and I know you think you are doing this for me but this isn't the way to go about it! Just because I'm not as good as him now doesn't mean that I never will be. I'll get there eventually… but only with your help," Marc said, slowly approaching his father.

"Please dad, let him go, you know this isn't the way!"

"I am so sorry! You know I would never hurt anyone," sobbed Jon as he dropped the knife and fell to his knees crying.

Marc ran towards his dad to comfort him.

"I just wanted this so badly for you," Jon said.

"Alex, Ian, let's go," said Miella, placed an arm around their shoulders and guided them out of the room.

On the way out they passed a couple stewards who were working in the stadium and told them there was a man needing help in their changing room.

"It's just constant drama with the two of you, isn't it?" Kaia said, trying to lighten the mood.

"I know tell me about it! I am seriously shocked by what has just happened there," replied Alex.

"Oh my gosh… he held a knife on me!" Ian said, in a state of shock.

"Look… I need for you both to do one thing for me... forget everything that just happened. You need to in order to win this race, we'll talk about it after. The bottom line is that you are both ok, nothing has happened to either of you physically to prevent you from winning. If you let what has just happened affect you, then he'll have won!"

"Del's right! Just go out there and win, you both know you can, so make sure you do," added Kaia.

"I promise the both of you, as a thank you for all that you have done in the last month, that we can and will do it!" Alex said, with Ian nodding in agreement.

"That's exactly what I wanted to hear!" Miella said.

"Indeed!" agreed Kaia.

True to their words, Ian finished first in his race and as soon as Alex crossed the finishing line first for his race, Kaia and Miella both felt their creators vibrate in their pockets at exactly the same time. They put their hands in their pockets and pulled out the creators that had somehow turned into mobile phones. They answered the call,

"Miella and Kaia, this is Zophia. Congratulations you have now completed your assignment successfully. Please return to Ricon immediately."

The line then went dead.

"Can't we go and congratulate them?"

"I don't know, Zophia did say immediately," replied Miella.

They looked over at Alex and Ian who were surrounded by photographers, TV crews, journalists and their parents. The boys looked up and saw Kaia and Miella watching them and signalled for them to join them.

Miella and Kaia both gave them the thumbs up and clapped. Miella then pointed at her watch, mouthed, 'Sorry we have to go,' and then pointed towards the exit.

Ian smiled and mouthed 'Thank you,' back at them. It was almost as if he knew they were there just to help them win the race.

Miella and Kaia smiled back and then disappeared amongst the crowd to find a suitable place to zel back to Ricon.

… … …

Ceremony Day

I

The two of them arrived back on Ricon to the sound of applause from the other trainees and their mentors.

"Congratulations! We are so proud of all of you," beamed Tilly.

"Excellent work! You completed this assignment like true Riconians. We are honoured to have you all on board," said Christopher.

"Well done," Tania said, hugging them all one by one.

"Oh, as usual it's up to Appie to break the bad news."

The children's expressions immediately changed from being happy to looks of concern.

"Oh Appie, stop being so dramatic and winding them up," said Tilly, laughing.

"Ok, ok! All I wanted to say is you have one hour to get ready and meet us outside the main hall for the Ceremony."

"Huh, so soon?" Patricia asked.

"Of course! Why waste time? There's another group of trainees who completed their assignments yesterday. We decided it would be best for all of you to graduate together and made the necessary arrangements. OK, I now make it fifty-six minutes and counting..." laughed Appie.

"What are we supposed to wear?" Ilene asked excitedly.

"You will find what you need laid out for you on your beds. If I were you I'd get going immediately," said Tilly.

"OK, enough said, we're off," replied Conor zeling back to his room with the others following immediately after.

II

They found lying on their beds, for the Ceremony, the Riconian Warrior uniform; cream trousers and cream long-sleeved, v-necked tops, made from a silky loose fitting type of material. Next to the trousers and top was a silver sash with instructions on how it should be tied, on the right, so that a knot formed a kind of pocket to hold their creators.

At the front of the bed was their footwear. Kaia looked at his, hesitant at first to put them on, as he thought they looked like ballet shoes or girl's slippers. They were made from the same silky material as the clothes and had barely visible rubber grips on the soles.

He put them on and looked at himself in the mirror. The outfit didn't look as bad as he thought it would. In fact it reminded him a lot of the fighters he used to watch in martial arts films with his dad.

He walked out of the room and tapped on Miella's bedroom door. She opened it,

"Wow! You look so cool!"

"You too! I feel as though I am about to enter a kung-fu competition dressed like this," said Kaia.

"Funny you say that, I was thinking the same," replied Miella. "Kaia, look at what I found lying next to my uniform," said Miella, holding out the picture her father took on the boat.

Kaia took hold of it and sat down on her bed. Miella sat down next to him.

"Look, we're back in the picture, how does that make you feel?"

"I really don't know what to feel, if I am to be completely honest! I know we have to forget the past in order to be here but that isn't always possible. Sometimes I think about them and about life as it was back then and I do miss it. I especially miss mum and dad!" Kaia admitted.

"That's exactly how I feel too. So much has happened here that I haven't had much time to think about it, but when I do get the odd moment, I remember our family and want to go back!"

"Miella, I think I am making the right decision. I feel as though I am really doing something good, and feel so alive here. I miss mum and dad like crazy but I know that in the long-term I'm better off here.

If I thought they were missing us and upset because they thought we had died on the boat then I would never have accepted this challenge but the fact is they are fine and happy with their lives without us and I'm ok, knowing that!"

"Me too, Kaia. As long as you're with me, I'm ready to let go of our old lives. Maybe not completely, but I won't get upset about it anymore. I'm just going to accept that this is the way things have turned out and they are like this for a reason, a good reason at that!"

There was a knock on the door. Miella got up and opened the door.

"Sorry to interrupt but we are all ready and wondering whether we should wait for you two or meet you outside the Ceremony Room?" Prashan asked.

Kaia looked at Miella for an answer.

"I'm ready to go and become a Riconian, how about you Kaia?"

"If you are, then so am I!" Kaia carefully placed the picture on Miella's bed. The pair of them then walked towards the door where Prashan was standing and firmly closed the door.

All six of them were now gathered together in the corridor,

"I guess this is it! I still can't get my mind around the fact that we are here. It's been crazy but fun! I can't get over how much has happened! We have all changed so much after everything that we have gone through. I'm glad to have done this with all of you," said Conor.

"I doubt I'm wrong in saying this, but I think we all feel the same," replied Prashan.

"No, you're right. I've had a wonderful time and consider all of you as great friends. I just really want you all to know that, please don't forget it," added Patricia

"Eugh... enough of the mushy-ness! Let's go and meet our mentors!" Kaia said light-heartedly.

They all zeled together and arrived outside the door of the Ceremony Room to find other children waiting there, dressed in the same outfits as them.

"Hi! You must all be from the other group graduating along with us today. I'm Janet, nice to meet you," said a very pretty blonde haired and blue eyed girl. "This is Joanna and next to her are Idalina, Robena, Maria, Kevin and Charlie-Joel, or CJ as he likes to be known," she continued.

Tilly suddenly appeared in the hallway with another person.

"My group, I would like to introduce you to another Riconian leader, Therese. She was Head Mentor for this group, and of course all of you know me.

Wow, don't you all look smart in your uniform, soon you'll have gold sashes and wings just like us... anyway, let's get going, follow me," said Tilly as she walked down the corridor.

"Ok, this door leads straight to the stage. The room is packed full of Riconians in the audience, on stage are Zophia, Candace and Harpz.

When we join them, Therese and I'll walk on ahead, all of you are to follow behind in a single file. Look directly ahead of you until we stop to turn and face the audience. Once that has happened, listen carefully to Zophia as she will guide you through the rest of the Ceremony, ok?"

They all nodded nervously.

"There's just one thing I would like to add; smile and enjoy yourselves as this is your big moment," said Therese.

"Ok, let's go!" said Tilly as she opened the door and walked up a few golden steps that led directly to the stage.

As soon as she stepped out, there was a very loud cheer and a lot of applause. Tilly stopped when reached the other end of the stage and turned her head slightly, just enough to make sure everyone was behind her, as instructed. She then turned to face the Riconian Warriors in the audience and the trainees copied her actions.

It was a sight Miella decided she would never forget. The room was lit-up brightly with hundreds of Riconians clapping loudly with their wings on display. Miella saw Appie, Christopher and Tania in the front row smiling proudly and clapping. There were two empty seats next to Appie that Tilly and Therese were now walking towards.

Zophia stepped out in front of the children and made a gesture with her hands asking for the audience to sit down, which they duly did. The room fell silent.

"It gives me an enormous amount of pleasure to be standing here in front of all of you, yet again, with some very special young people. They have all successfully completed their challenges and are now more than worthy to join us as Riconian Warriors.

Before you became trainees, you were promised the option of returning home if you felt this wasn't a path you wished for your lives. Is there is anyone who would now like to take up that option?" Zophia asked.

All the trainees looked around at each other nervously to see if anyone would change their minds. Nothing was said.

"Great we can now..."

"STOP!" Patricia shouted.

"I am really, really sorry, and I feel as though I am letting everyone down by saying this, but I can't do it," she said, with tears streaming down her face.

Miella looked at the faces of everyone else in her group. She could see they were all just as stunned by Patricia's actions and decision as she was. She looked down in the audience and could also see the disappointment on Tilly, Appie, Tania and Christopher's faces.

"I have had an amazing time here and I know that by returning to Earth I will no longer remember any of it... but I feel as though my parents need me just as much, if not more, than anyone else.

I also feel as though I am letting everyone here down and for that I am truly sorry," she said looking at her wrist and touching her gold bracelet.

"Not at all Patricia, it takes a lot for you to make a decision like that and to be able to say it in front of all of us, in this situation can only mean that it is the right thing for you to do. We all have a great amount of respect for you in doing that. If you wish, you may say a quick goodbye to your fellow trainees before I send you back," replied Zophia.

Appie stood up and started clapping his hands. He was soon joined by all the other Riconians in the audience.

Whilst this was going on, Patricia gave Miella, Kaia, Conor, Ilene and Prashan a quick and teary hug goodbye. She then took her place next to Zophia. Zophia smiled at Patricia, wiped the tears from her eyes, gave her a hug and then zeled her out of the room.

As soon as Patricia disappeared everyone sat down and went back to being silent.

"As you have all just seen, we have sadly lost one of our recruits but happily, we still have more who wish to join us... so without seeing any further reason to delay this process, I'll now proceed in giving these trainees their wings and making them Riconian Warriors.

Zophia stepped behind Kaia and instantly created some wings. She placed them just below Kaia's shoulder blades and pushed gently. Kaia felt a comfortable and nice heat travel from that spot and spread throughout his body. At the same time, a warm glow of light appeared around him and his creator started flashing and changing into all of the colours it had previously been until it stopped at red. As soon as it stopped, the sash around Kaia's waist went from silver to gold.

Zophia then did the same to all the other trainees.

As soon as they had all received their wings, Zophia looked at them and said,

"Congratulations, you are now all Riconian Warriors but as you know your journey has only just begun!"

... ...

Author's Note:

Thank you to all my friends and family who have supported and encouraged me whilst writing this book and trying to get it published! There are however, a few people I need to thank individually:

Candace Cort, thanks for reading the first two chapters and encouraging me to continue writing.

Ilene Hardy, thanks so much for your support throughout and helping me name the book.

Tamsin "Tilly" Garrity, thanks for your patience and perseverance in helping me edit this. You are a saint and true friend.

Harpreet "Harpz" Nagra, my 'soul-sister', thank you for all of your support.

Eliane Stephens-Falconi, thank you for all of your encouragement, help and not letting me lose faith.

Christine Pamintuan, great work on the website: www.childrenofricon.com and thanks for helping to create the book cover. Tania Nadarajah, Charles Maurice and Conor Holohan, thanks to you guys too for your help with the cover.

Shaney Blackman, thanks for the excellent photography for the website.

In addition to those above, I want to say thanks to:
Maria and Julian Emmanuel, Ellena & Felician Emmanuel, Fabian Emmanuel, Marc Emmanuel, Silvia Martina, Joanna Mastrides, Bettina Weitzer, Kathryn Allen, Ian Timis, Idalina DeSousa, Natalie Rowell, Tamara Gibson, Fieldman 'Superhero' Robinson, Janet Isokariari, Michelle Olorunda, Angela Manso, NTL friends – Thelma, Cassie, Fatama, Lani, David, Michael, Greg aka Flo, Omega, Neera & Pinal, Lucy Slater, Cicero Tucker, The Amalans – Therese, Hary & Aruna, John Bailey, David Wills, Caroline Nash, Nadia Hardman, Nav Nagra, Demetrios Bradshaw, Aunts – Theo, Dina, Patricia & Usha, Charlotte Campbell, Martin Giraud and Robena Tejedor for all your support and for not letting me give up on this!

Finally, Idalina... thanks for your excellent choice in names and for the best present ever x

Printed in the United Kingdom by
Lightning Source UK Ltd., Milton Keynes
138846UK00002B/5/P